Goodwyn Barmby

The Return of the Swallow

And other Poems

Goodwyn Barmby

The Return of the Swallow
And other Poems

ISBN/EAN: 9783744770750

Printed in Europe, USA, Canada, Australia, Japan

Cover: Foto ©Andreas Hilbeck / pixelio.de

More available books at **www.hansebooks.com**

THE

RETURN OF THE SWALLOW

AND OTHER POEMS

THE

RETURN OF THE SWALLOW

AND OTHER POEMS

BY .

GOODWYN BARMBY

Author of "The Poetry of Home and Childhood," &c.

LONDON:

SIMPKIN, MARSHALL, & CO.

1864.

PRINTED BY JOHN HAMER, LEEDS.

NOTICE.

——•——

THE RETURN OF THE SWALLOW is now for the first time published. THE SCENES OF SPRING have before been issued, in pamphlet form, but are now revised. Of the MISCELLANEOUS POEMS, some are new, others appeared in the pages of popular periodicals about ten years ago. With the exception, then, of THE POETRY OF HOME AND CHILDHOOD, a new edition of which will be soon forthcoming, this is a general collection of my verses.

GOODWYN BARMBY.

WESTGATE PARSONAGE, WAKEFIELD.
July, 1864.

CONTENTS.

THE RETURN OF THE SWALLOW.

THE SCENES OF SPRING.

POEMS.

CONTENTS.

CONTENTS.

THE

RETURN OF THE SWALLOW

The Return of the Swallow.

A POEM.

PART I.

THE RIVER SIDE.

IT was a lovely day in June,—
The year's mid-day, and day's own noon;
The sun was high above the hills,
Thin through the meadows ran the rills,
And, hot and weary, with a shiver,
Dived in the coolness of the river,
Which flowed between its banks and woods—
Those many-peopled solitudes--

B

As quietly, and cool, and clear,
As a good life flows through a year;
Of many hues of shade and sun,
All equable, and calm, and one.

Amid the glass of that fair stream,
The shapes of trees, the grasses' gleam,
And the rich hues of the bank-flowers,
Shone clearly in those noontide hours;
While 'neath the shadow of the wood,
Two human forms together stood:
The twin reflections which they gave
Mirrored within the flowing wave,
And rising with its rippled run,
And blent in liquid unison.

What curve of grace, what poise of sweep,
Enters that sphere of stillness deep,
Eddies the calmness of the air,
And moves the human gazers there?
Who upward turn, and earnest note
A light form through the æther shoot,—
The substance of a sudden shade,
Which swiftly o'er their eyeballs played,

As, veering in, a swallow's flight
Specked with dark wing those waters bright,
Like purple bud snapped from a spray,
Cast on a stream, and borne away.

On flew the visitant of spring,
Bearing the summer on its wing,
As o'er a lake a pinnace frail
Might skim the waves with sloping sail;
And now the quick sweep of its wing
Veered its bright bark in many a ring,—
Its tail the rudder, and its head
The prow, which swiftly onward sped,
Cleaving the warm tides of the air
With fragrance sweet and sun-sparks fair,
Casting the shimmering sunshine back,
Gilding its plumes upon its track,
And moving on, in circuits wide,
Rippling with light the aëry tide.

On flew the swallow from their sight,
Following the river's line of light.
And now its arrowy wing would dip
Amid the stream, as though to sip

The cups of bubbles bursting fair,
Or touch its shadow floating there.
And now, in higher curves, its wing
Would sweep forth in a wider ring,
And, slanting to the sunshine, show
A silvery light and purple glow,
The bloom of its soft plumage shed
Upon the eye from overhead :
A shifting show of dark and bright,
The glow of gloom and glance of light.

Beside the stream were pastures green,
And cornfields rich, and many a scene
Of uplands tressed with clustering trees,
And bank-flowers glowing on the breeze.
Grazing the herbage, thick and dank,
Fringing the steep sides of the bank,
The uddered kine and heifers light,
Showed their bright flanks of red and white,
Painting the air, and in the stream
Reflected through inverting beam—
The river-shadows, breast to breast,
With their bank-neighbours couched at rest,
Or with each other, hoof to hoof,
Cropping the self-same grassy woof—

Those on the bank, within the stream
Reversed, as in a world of dream :
Yet o'er them both the swallow flew,
Unconscious which were false or true.

Now skimming lightly by the cove,
Where the rare water-lilies move
Their gold and silver cups, and leaves
Which, heart-like, throb in graceful heaves,
As runs the river heedless by,—
The swift bird takes the bright-winged fly :
A moment sparkling in the air,
Then gone, as pleasures coloured fair
Vanish in the consuming sigh
Of swiftly-passing destiny.

And now the banks with flowers are flush,
And, lover-like, the waters blush ;
As where, like nymph, the long grass likes
To lave its locks, their rosy spikes
Crimson the stream and flow in dyes
As rich as those from sunset skies.
And now the blue vetch hangs its curls,
Where round a bend the water whirls,

Purpling the ripples as they run,
To break amid the sedge-roots dun.
The umbels of the hemlock now
Their melancholy shadows throw ;
And now the graceful meadow-sweet
Shines in the stream, with motion fleet
Shaking its tresses, like a nymph
Bathing amid that mirrory lymph.
And now, where higher shelves the shore,
A leafy wood the flood looks o'er,
While in the stream itself—another
Grows downward, like as own twin brother :
Its form the same, yet dim and thin
As ghosts of trees which once had been.
Its branches spectral, and its leaves
Such skeletons as autumn weaves,
When the green flesh it takes away,
And shreds the leaf and browns the spray.
Yet, in the wave, that wood-piece seemed
Restored to life, when o'er it gleamed
The swallow's shade, as though it flew
Its branching ashy arches through.

The river now, in shallower bed,
Between some dreary marshes sped.

Yet still the bird flew with the stream,
While played the fly with tempting beam ;
And fishes, with ambition rash,
Leaped in the air and fell with splash—
As hasty souls, on high spheres bent,
Fail out of their own element.

By the marsh-sides, the globe-flower bright
Displayed its orb, with gilding dight ;
Upon the air the flowering rush,
Bending its frail head, sent its blush ;
And yellow irises in bands,
.Stood, soldier-like, with bristling brands,
Yet shone in bloom, as though the shoots
Of sunshine burst from forth their roots.

Guarding the river's shallow edges,
Arrayed with plumes were ranked the sedges ;
While angry looked the crimson mallows,
And mournful drooped the silvery sallows,
As constant never, changing ever,
The current neared them but to sever ;
And onward flow, with fiercer force,
By other banks, in narrower course.

Between grey boulders, rising dry,
The stream swirled its dark waters by;
Then flowed o'er layers, where each boss
Of earth's stone shields was red with moss,
Or green with cressy growths, whose dyes
Colour the stream, as o'er it flies
The arrowy swallow, shooting low
Beneath each over-hanging bough,
And almost dipping, as to quaff,
Where ran the ripples with a laugh,
Made of all merry, child-like trebles,
Over the shining rounded pebbles,
Which gleamed like brown eyes, when the beam
Of love's sweet smile gilds sorrow's stream,
And shows the fractures, glancing bright
'Mid waters dark, of clefts of light.

A mill dam now the stream restrained,
Which flowed like courser, torrent-maned,
Bitted its foaming mouth, nor feared
To rein it in until it reared;
Then, in wild gallop o'er the wheel,
Scattered its spray with ringing peal
Of falling waters, and the clash
Of silvery sounds, and diamonds flash,

And rainbow gleams of amethyst
And ruby, crowned with shining mist.

And now the swallow turned its neck,
And left the channel of the beck—
Its sliding run and shining level,
Its foamy fall and sprayey revel,
Its hurrying stream, and woody sides—
To wing the air, as fancy guides.

Over the scented haysel meadows,
On whose mown sward spread lengthy shadows :
O'er ridged grass here, and haycocks there,
Just freshly cut or bleaching fair,
With many varied dyes of green,
And shades where the blue blade had been—
The swallow flew with twittering throat,
In chorus with the scythe's keen note.

Over a village, where a patch
Of low white houses, roofed with thatch,
Beneath a wood's green spreading boughs,
Its life upon the landscape throws ;—

Over a pond, where knee-deep stand
The uddered kine, with look so bland,
And with such meditative grace
In each large eye and pensive face;—
Along a road, whose dusty line
Shows white between its hedges fine;—
Beside a stack-yard, where a muster
Of yellow-ricks, in thick group cluster;—
Over a brown barn, and long shed,
Whence glanced the cattle's flanks of red;—
Around an outhouse, whence the cotes
Of pigeons gave forth cooing notes;
While some blue-wings and ring-necks fair,
Rose high in flight amid the air,
A moment poised, and quickly then
Went o'er and o'er to earth again;—
Over a farmstead, where the roof
Was piled with chimneys, high aloof,
From whence the rising curls of smoke
The harshness of the outline broke;—
O'er orchard near, where shone with play
The apple-cheeks of children gay;—
Around the grey tower of a church,
Its pointing spire and antique porch;—
In circling flight the swallow sped,
While over every scene it shed

The presence of a spirit bright,
A sense of love and gleam of light.

And now the shades began to glance ;
And the grey gnats were at their dance ;
The birds flew upward to their roosts ;
Was heard the buzz of insect hosts ;
The miller-moths their white wings try,
And flit like ghosts of butterfly ;
The marsh hens cluck in the reeds, and shoot
From grassy bank and willow root ;
And a dim mist, with wavy wreath,
Hangs o'er the river underneath,
As o'er again the swallow swept
Where the ambitious grayling leapt :
Then veered again with curving wing,
And floated round in wider ring,
Where still two forms within the stream
Reflected are with blended gleam ;
A manly shape ; a virgin face ;
A noble brow ; a glance of grace ;
The youth and maid, who since noon-tide
Have loitered by that river-side.

O, ask not why so long had stood,
Those twain, beside that sheltering wood !

O, ask not why so sweet their dream,
Straying beside that shining stream !
O, ask not why their best loved mood,
Is to seek each in solitude !
Hast thou not known the hours fly by
Like instants, in a loved one's eye ?
Hast thou not known a world of woe,
In a swift dream forgotten go ?
Hast thou not known a throng so dull,
When absent her—thy beautiful ?
And felt the best society
Was having her alone with thee ?
Hast thou not known, hast thou not heard,
The coo of love's fair ring-necked bird ?
Then, ask not why, beside that stream,
While time has flitted like its gleam,
Telling their love, have stayed so long
The youth and maiden of our song.

" Behold," said he, as overhead
Again the bird its circuit sped,
" That swallow, circling in the air,
And round and round us flying there,
To the same place from whence it flew,
It will restore its purple hue;

Mark how it circles in its flight,
And brings us back its silver bright !
What equal curves its long wings keep,
In narrower or in wider sweep !
I should not doubt, that this same day,
That bird has winged ten miles away,
And is this evening now returning
To where it pruned itself this morning !
And thus, when summer fades away,
And leaves these heavens clouded grey,
A wider circuit it will take,
And to the south its voyage make :
Then here return, when days grow long,
With summer bloom and summer song.
And surely as that swallow flies
Back to this stream from southern skies,
Seeks its old haunts, and skims again
This lovely river-thridded plain :
So will thy Gerald happy come
Back to his Bertha and his home,
When, rising from this old year's urn,
Another summer sun shall burn."

She smiled upon him, with such looks
As make men wiser far than books,

Then playfully she said : " Thy word
Were better far without thy bird.
The bonny thing !—I love it well,—
May never leave its English dell,
But, weak in wing and ware of flight,
Sleep torpid through the winter's night :
Or on its voyage blown aside,
Perish upon the briny tide ;
Or on some Norland promontory,
Pine in the cold, and end its story.
For you I trust the fates devise
A summer under Tuscan skies ;
A chesnut grove and bower of vines,
Beneath the purple Apennines ;
And all the arts of hue and form
Can clear to calm, or swell to storm ;
So that, like some fair southern cape,
Your colouring moulds itself to shape,
And you bring back to our white shore,
The voice to sing and wing to soar."

" Dearest," said he, " thy wish shall be
The breath of a true prophecy ;
Yet, O believe me, that bright bird,
Whose twitter overhead is heard,

Shall be my chosen messenger,
And prove my advent, like a star,
When it shall northward come once more,
I hail again my Bertha's door ;
The winter will sufficient be,
This time, for Art and Italy ;
With what flush Autumn liberal throws,
Of rich fruit-stains and sunset glows :
And what the early spring may yield
Of budding wood and sprouting field.
O bird of wheeling wing and flight,
Which sweeps around in circles bright !
Bird, whose return next year shall bring
Another summer on thy wing !
With thee I go, with thee come back ;
Thy fate is mine, and thine my track ;
Thy plumes the spicy scents shall bear,
And my soul gather fragrance there !"

To Italy ! to grow in art,
And better act the painter's part ;
Beneath its purple sky to stand,
And draw its blueness to his hand ;
Amid its dazzling light to dip
His brush, and cast on beauty's lip ;

In its pine forests far to roam,
And for his canvas drink their gloom.
To Italy ! to learn the charm
That rounded lay on carven arm ;
The loitering loveliness to trace,
That dimpled in a sculptured face ;
The force to own, the soul to feel,
The marble rended to reveal ;
With shapes of power the mind to fill,
And watch the stone grow strong in will ;
The features fix and swell the chest,
The muscles strain and heaven contest ;
Or flower in beauty, with a head
Of maiden locks, like hyacinths spread.
Such Gerald's aim, that he might store
His mind with forms from Art's bright shore,
And bring to England's pallid skies
The wealth and warmth of southern dyes ;
That he might claim, by well-earned fame,
To blend with his, his Bertha's name,
And greet their union with the dower,
Of work of skill and sense of power.

O bitter sweet, the hour of parting,
When eyes are down-cast—tears are starting.

And e'en the fire of passion flashes
'Neath the wet fringes of the lashes—
When on your shoulder broad is laid,
The pale brow of your timid maid,
And, guarding her with circling arm,
You plead the woe, yet bless its charm!
While she, O sweet soul! quite forgets
Her many dues amid her debts,
Owes you a thousand thoughts away,
And pays beforehand while you stay;
And when for absent years you mourn,
In months anticipates return!
O bitter sweet, the hour which parted
The loving, gallant, and right-hearted!
Such praise to Gerald, song must render,
From Bertha, trusting, true, and tender!
Yet that the breasts of lovers fold,
Should never unto all be told,—
Its mystery and its grace are such,
You dim to breathe, you soil to touch.
Over their parting blue mists fell,
And sweet sounds stilled their fond farewell.

PART II.

THE CAMPAIGN.

HE eve was fine, the cloudland bright
   With dazzling waves of amber light,
      And crimson isles, with cliff and tree,
   Seemed floating in that golden sea,
   While, crowned with many a mountain head,
   A purple continent far spread :
   Its shores with spires and turrets gay,
A ruby cape and amethyst bay,
And through it swept, like robe of Scald,
A lake of living emerald ;
And in its midst a city beamed,
With walls that shone and gates that gleamed

With all the shooting rays of gems
That light our New Jerusalems.

Amid that sunset's gorgeous blaze,
Its shifting, glancing, glowing rays,
Like jewel sparks of purple gleam,
The swallows quivered in the beam,
Shooting as swift as glancing stars
Towards the heavens' golden bars,
As though no flight would ever tire
Their wings of wind and souls of fire.

And when the evening greyer grew,
And green hills melted into blue,
And in the west that cloudland bright
Had flaked in saffron streaks of light,
The swallows, twittering with wild glee,
Still circled o'er the grassy lea :
Wheeling around the high church tower,
Trying in flight their young ones' power,
And round and round, till day was gone,
In ceaseless curves sped flying on ;
And then, with many a lesser ring,
And anxious cry and rustling wing,

On the old tower alit in mass,
Eager the darkness swift should pass.

Hast ever seen amid the east,
While Hesper pales like white-robed priest,
That momentary glance of light,
Which of morn's coming warns the night?
It woke the swallows, twittering loud
And gathering in a glooming cloud,
And soon as the true morning broke
In column close their flight they took;
A wedge-like phalanx, bearing brave
Through air, and casting back its wave,
By the early labourer just seen,
A cloud of shade, in sky serene :
And with the swallow Gerald went,
Each south, their flight and fortunes blent.

He passed the Alp and Apennine,
The tinted snow, the elm-bound vine;
The field of many an ancient story,
The marbled town of time-stained glory,
The river with its mountain swell,
The convent with its tinkling bell,

The trellised grapes, the orange grove,
The wide-horned oxen's shaggy drove,
The peasant with his sheep-skin suit,
His ribboned hat and pastoral flute,
The historic way, the ruined tomb,
The heathen temple's chequered gloom,
Amid whose broken columns grey
The transient gleams of radiance play,
Like youth round age ; while myrtle springs
From fissured block, and cicale sings—
Like the new life which then was springing,
And the new song which then was ringing
From heart to heart, and strand to strand,
Of that old Imperial land,—
The full deep-bosomed Italy—
The Italy that should be free,—
Wakening woman, wakening man,
From Messina to Milan ;
Shaking Rome's old priestcraft hoary,
Rousing heroes for new story ;
Causing ghosts of ages past
To leave their tombs and rise at last :
While midst the storm a state rose free,
Like crystal city from the sea.

A spark of that most sacred fire
Lit up his soul, and made a pyre
Of all unholy passions there,
And glowed like lamp by altar fair.
He joined the chieftain at whose word
Slaves leapt to men, and vows were heard
Which Heaven chronicled, and gave
As victory's war-cries to the brave,
And legends for the coming time
To illustrate in hue and rhyme !
He joined the chieftain by whose powers
True hearts were drawn, as light draws flowers ;
And where his red shirt gleamed, as Mars
With ruddy flame beams mid the stars,
And shone the orb of victory,
First of the foremost there was he !

O say not that he erred, to take
The sword, and fight for freedom's sake,
In other lands than that dear one,
Where first he saw the rising sun ;
O blame him not !   In one red flood
Flows the great brotherhood of blood.
The love of freedom is the same,
Where'er 'tis felt, whate'er its name.

The daring prompt to rise and stand
In battle for your native land,
With foot amid the surges' roar
To hurl the invader from your shore ;
Or, beaten back, the strength which wills
To die in fight upon your hills ;
From the same generous passion spring,
Are pinioned from the same bright wing,
Which bears a brother from one land,
To aid those of another strand
To gain their freedom, and to stone
The cruel tyrant from his throne ;
For Liberty itself is one
In every clime beneath the sun,
And tyrants, selfish, stupid, blind,
Are the fell foes of all mankind.
Then blame him not, that in his hand
He lifted an Italian brand,
And where he heard the cry of woe
Rushed on to rescue and o'erthrow !
The wrongs of others on us call ;
Our rights, they are the rights of all ;
The cause of freedom and of worth,
Alike the cause of all the earth !

And where was now the painter's part?
And where was Gerald's work of art,
To which he vowed Italian days,
And dreamt upon his Bertha's praise?
Forgotten not!—and yet laid by,
As thing profane, though with a sigh!
For each fond task, each dear-loved plan,
Seemed mean beside the work of man:
Creation of the citizen,
And manufacture of free men;
And brighter than the painter's easel,
And grander than the sculptor's chisel,
Unto him gleamed the patriot's sword,
Before him beamed the battle's lord;
For though, as with a burst of tone,
The image white leapt from the stone,
And all but lived;—how greater when
From dullest clay sprang living men,
And moved in masses, like swift bands
Of angels with redeeming hands,—
No more the children of the sod,
But heaven-turned heads and sons of God!

O little seems the act of art,
When human interests claim the heart;

When tyrants rage and subjects yield,
'Tis poor to paint the battle-field.
When slaves arise, and foes are flying,
Vain work to limn the hues of dying!
When Freedom calls, O who would trace
The colour mantling in her face?
Better to scale the foeman's banks,
In the red glow of rushing ranks:
To mingle in the light that jets
From the wild gleam of bayonets;
To follow Freedom's coloured cloud,—
The flag of conquest, or your shroud!

But what of Love? Could freedom's flame
Burn out the print of Bertha's name,
On Gerald's heart engraven deep
As veins in rocks of Calpe's steep?
Ah, no! True love and freedom dwell
In union indestructible;
And freedom's love from love is born,
And both all selfish motives scorn;
And warmer, from a gallant blow,
Would Gerald's heart for Bertha glow.

Up the white road of rising lands,
Marched on the liberating bands;

Two rows of Lombard poplars, tall,
Bordered it with a verdant wall;
Then, as they rose, from ledge to ledge,
The aloes massed them in a hedge;
And rolling stones, with frantic leap,
Came bounding down the arid steep;
Whose summit gained—a transient glance
Was cast around the broad expanse
Of vale and mountain, stream and wood,
Black lava track and lake's bright flood,
Which, grateful for their flowing rills,
Mirrored the grandeur of the hills,
As o'er its molten surface bright
A swallow glanced with curving flight,
And sent the thoughts of Gerald back
Quickly upon his English track,
Awakening memories of that stream
Where last he shared his sweet love-dream,
And made that bird a pledge serene,
His Bertha and himself between,
On whose wing memory's light should burn—
The harbinger of his return!

And where was Bertha? Did she think
Of him who marched to Danger's brink?

And could she blame him, and regret
The gleam of the fell bayonet?
Or think him either rash or wrong,
To aid the weak against the strong?
He judged her better than to deem
Her thought would flow in such thin stream,
And knew that nothing could distress
Love more, than thought of selfishness.
When first he joined the war of right
He wrote her of the tidings bright
In words of hope, and planned a story
Of freedom's rise and future glory:
Such as inspired, with valour's tread,
All those whom Garibaldi led:
As when beneath a noble arch
We raise our heads and stately march;
Or, to the measure of a hymn,
Accord the pulse and move the limb.
But since, he had not heard from her
Amid the wild life and the stir
Of the red conflict: blown back hair
Of battle here and victory there;
The rally swift, and swelling large,
The torrent fury of the charge;
The close set teeth of triumph's bruit,
And the strained eyes of fierce pursuit!

To her, once more, the swallow's flight
Sent back his thoughts in vision bright.
He saw her by the river's brim,
Where last they met, in thought of him ;
Bertha, the bright—all blush, all bloom,
A flower of radiance and perfume !
Bertha, the good—with smiles divine
For each good wish or act benign !
Bertha, the kind—whose tears would start
Pure, from the fountains of her heart !
Bertha, the fond—whose love was given
To him alone, beneath dear heaven ;
Bertha, the plighted—whose pledged word
Was sure as the returning bird !

He could not doubt ; his faith in her
Was like the seaman's in the star !
And blessed is he, who, 'mid the storm,
Can see the skirts of angel form,
And, midst the stress of incidence,
Grasp the bright hem of Providence,
And wave, in battle with the world,
The banner woman has unfurled !
Yea, blessed is he, who goes to war
By woman armed in freedom's car ;

Who feels he has with him the life
Of woman—mother, daughter, wife ;
And knows he claims, at danger's call,
Her glance to shine, her tear to fall ;
Curst by defeat, by victory blest,
Her sigh to soothe, her smile to rest !

Blessed, in the faith of Bertha's truth
And constant love, marched on the youth :
Now speeding past the trellised vines,
Now climbing through the mountain pines ;
Then, when the long-forced march was done,
Basking with lizards in the sun,
Or watching the fleet swallows quiver,
And dreaming of an English river.

Yet, where's the soul of such mean birth
Which values not historic earth ?
In Italy, what foot could fall,
Where graves would not resound the call,
And send back answer from beneath,
Like music from the lips of death ?
What heap of stones embrowned and dry
But formed some city's turrets high ?

What column, with acanthus bound,
But pillared some wide temple round ?
What fig-tree wild, or red-limbed vine,
Or ilex bright, or spreading pine,
But nourished, grew, and raised its head
O'er ashes of the immortal dead ?
The very clay had once a name,
The very dust had Roman fame :
And when wind-eddied o'er the hill,
To thought it had a glory still !

On, on, they marched !   The tyrant fled
As mist before the wind is sped,
Yet rallied for last struggle fell,
As at its furthest darkens hell,
And from the abysm of its lair
Shows crunching teeth and eyes that glare
With red fire-light ; and horrent hair,
And claws that rend and tusks that tear.

How rarely is the day all fine,
From its dim dawn to its decline !
As dark meets bright on pheasant's breast,
So golden east brings gloaming west ;

And brightly though the day begun,
Yet cloudily its course is run ;
The rosy petals of the morn
By the wind's fingers rudely torn—
The sun, with saffron tresses shed,
Setting with face of angry red !

Thus fine the morn, when Gerald rose
Alert to march against his foes ;
The eve thus stormy, when he fell
Pierced with the splinter of a shell ;
So eager, too, his dawn of strife,
So swift his close of soldier's life :
At morn, with all health's bravest signs ;
At eve, brought fainting to his lines !
And wan and bleeding borne away
To pallet poor, in convent grey.

O blessed and beautiful the blood
For Freedom poured, in generous flood !
O loved by God, whene'er it ran
In service for the weal of man !
O blessed the wounds received in front,
On the right side, in battle's brunt !

Who would not value above stars,
The trophies of their glorious scars?
And who not feel the crimson strife
Was sacred to the God of Life?
O blessed blood by martyrs shed!
O wounds of the immortal dead!
O glorious scars by heroes won,
Be yours mankind's best benison!
Yet many a nameless one has sighed
His life away in purple tide,
Without an eye to paint his need,
Without a pen to gild his deed,
Without a plaudit from Fame's tongue—
The peal of his renown unrung!
Glory to these—the nameless host—
The least who rank beside the most!
The last who by the first shall stand—
Glory to them in every land!
Arise, Bright Tomb! whereon is read—
" Unto the Nameless, Glorious Dead!"

Part III.

THE CONVENT.

———

LONG days and weary, Gerald lay
      With fractured limb, hot fever's prey;
      Now underneath the surgeon's hand,
   And now by Sister Nina fanned;
   At first—despaired of: wandering, wild—
   Sleepless, and babbling like a child,
Of shining stream and woody hollow,
Of maiden pale and floating swallow;
And then in silent swoon supine,
Stretched out without a life-like line
Of motion in his piteous face,—
Which yet had its own quiet grace,
As of a lake, so very still,
Deep 'neath the shadow of a hill.

D

Like light shed on a landscape dun,
Beamed o'er his couch the white-faced nun,
The Sister Nina, with pale hair
Drawn off a brow too sickly fair;
And hazel eyes, whose depth of dark,
Concentred in a fiery spark
Of vision, glowing and intense—
Piercing the spirit through the sense,
And from their orbs at once revealing
Thought's presence, and the power of feeling.

A kindly nurse! Her patient knew
Her tread before she moved in view,
So soft it came upon the ear,
As though love kept in step with fear;
And then her movements had a grace
His wandering eyes were pleased to trace,
E'er strength for speech returned, and skill
The phrase with grateful sense to fill.
Yes! she had watched while he was sleeping—
The vigils thus of mercy keeping;
Yes! when in his unconsciousness
She had thought for him; in the stress
Of pain and fever helping him
To bear out through the struggle dim,

And by kind glance and soothing palm
Had won his fretfulness to calm ;
Aiding his words as speech returned,
And in his cheeks their dawning burned,
With conscious looks and quick assent,
Or swift surmise—foreseen intent—
And all which readiness of will
Discerns of good, perceives of ill,
Anticipates for thought or sense,
And acts in part of Providence.

He was her charge ! The tyrant's shells
Had filled the other convent cells,
And of the sisterhood, each tried
To be of one the nurse and guide,
And happy Gerald, that some voice
Within had made that youth her choice ;
A voice of memory, which said—
" Like him who at Magenta bled !"—
Her brother, with the fair young head
There numbered with the noble dead !
And, for the likeness' sake, she deemed
She cared for him, nor ever dreamed
That woman's nature otherwise
Would stir her heart, or fill her eyes,

Or make her feel the spirit's strife—
Her unfilled round and void of life.

Not that she loved him in that fashion
Which makes of love a sense and passion;
As maid loves youth, or youth loves maiden—
Each with the weight of longing laden;
But that he woke within her spirit
A feeling dim, yet of such merit
She could but value it, a need
Of something unpossessed indeed,
Which pleased her while it yet was paining,
As fruits delight the lips they're staining,
And made her conscious of a sense
Unfilled: a void of joy intense,
Just found; yet a reality
Which might have been or yet might be.

Still was it round the convent wall,
So still, you heard a dry leaf fall;
So still, so silent, and so lone,
The slow drip on the fountain stone—
Its broken marble dank with green—
Came like a voice upon the scene!

So still, the starlings on the vane
Made of their chirps a hurricane!
So still, the grey tower's shadows thrown
Upon the ground showed masses brown!
So still, the poplars' waveless lines—
So still, the sombre clump of pines—
So still, the human thought and will—
Within those walls—so very still!
So still the tread of Nina's feet
That Gerald heard his own heart beat!

Her woman's interest soon had found
Way to his heart, and there unwound
The string of silence from his mouth,
As gushed from hers her own sweet south;
And then her ear received a tale
From lips and face with passion pale;
Then colouring red as ripening grape
Of Bertha's grace and Bertha's shape;
Her step so light—the grasshopper
Could scarcely spring away from her!
Her shape so slight—her form so fair,
Was scarce distinguished from the air,
Nor stained its crystal! Yes, she had
Colour, and so had clouds, as glad

They streaked with crimson blush the face
Of heaven, and gave its pureness grace ;
But she was not less crystalline
Than the air when filled with rich sunshine,
Or the garden of her face less fair,
Because a rosebud blossomed there !
Oh, then, she was perfection ? Yes !
She was complete and born to bless !
There was between them nothing dim—
No mist on their horizon's rim ;
They had been lovers from their youth—
They doubted not each other's truth,
But had love-grown as tendrils grow,
Or honeysuckles twine and blow,
Or sweetbriar roses cling together
From nearness, warmth, and sunny weather.

How beautiful ! the Sister said,
As o'er her face a bright tinge spread—
How beautiful to share such feeling,
And antedate the blest revealing
Of so much heaven on the earth,
In deathless love and holy mirth !
She wished him strength again, to meet
The glad looks of his mistress sweet,

And oped the lattice, that the air
Should find a playmate in his hair.
Poor lonely thing! it wandered wide,
And should not be shut out from pride;
With it a wish for health it brought,
And, like best blessings, came unsought:
Then let it in—its breath was mild,
And soft as of an infant child;
It told of spring's green buds and sprays,
Of travel home and happy days.

Alas! her thought would further reach
Than the scant confines of her speech,
Though modesty the finger tip
Of silence, pressed upon her lip,
And much she felt which, were it spoken,
Her heart for virgin pride were broken.
Why was she bound, and others free?
Was it Christ's yoke, or slavery—
A Gospel bond, or priestly chain—
A work of good, or doom of pain?
Surely the heavenly Mother smiled
On her, as on a chosen child;
Then why her misery? Was it sin,
And punishment for wrong within,

Or sin without which placed her there,
Shut out from Nature's circuits fair ;
Deprived of all the joy which, shared,
Grows not the less—by use impaired,
But swells the greater, growing strong
By practice, as rise prayer and song.
O, awful thought, to couple such !
And, O sad soul, such theme to touch !
Yet why the want within ? the chasm
Of being, rent in painful spasm ?
The void of soul—the rainbow ridge
Of heaven itself had failed to bridge ?
Why that response to Gerald's tale,
Which blanched her lips like lilies pale,
And pained her heart, while the thought, swift,
Came like red sun on white snow drift—
O could I love, to love how sweet !
O were I loved, what bliss complete !
O might I love—delicious pain !
O were I loved to love again !

    The very air was breath of fame,
Wide wafting Garibaldi's name
And sounds of freedom, on its way,
E'en to that convent's walls of grey ;

And its doors opened at that word,
And from its cage flew many a bird,
Glad of its liberty, to doff
Her garb, to put her dull suit off,
And moulting quick new plumes to don
And prune fresh feathers in the sun ;
Yet Nina stayed ; the fresh green shoot
Burst forth from many a darksome root ;
The ivy round the walls grew bright,
The vine stems wreathed in redder light ;
The hepaticas, in lowly cluster,
Shone gay with blue and crimson lustre ;
Their tender buds put forth the maples,
And liberty now reigned in Naples :
While all the new life of the spring
Seemed joyous for her welcoming.

The voice of freedom on the air—
The stir of new life everywhere,
To Gerald's nurse came wondrously,
She was, and yet she was not free !
Freedom called to her with a tongue,
In which her duty had not sung
Its hymns to Mary ; while her choice
Joyed in it as her country's voice ;

Yet Nina stayed.   The little birds
Chirped, Fly with us ! as though in words ;
The winds came over hill and hollow,
And cried, We go—come, follow, follow !
A busy gnat came buzzing by,
And whispered, Why, e'en I can fly !
An early bee its horn blew free,
And sung, Come, seek the flowers with me !
Yet Nina stayed; the ivy chill
So clung unto the ruin still,
Yet ever greener grew its shoots
And life was quickening at its roots.

O sad is slavery ! sad the chain
The limping negro drags with pain,
Over the rice swamps, when the gash
Is raw beneath the driver's lash !
O sad is slavery, when the brand
Of foreign tyrant smites the land
That once its rulers chose, and bends
Its body to his baser ends ;
Cuts out its tongue—forbids the reach
Of converse in its native speech ;
Rends from its back its raiment fair—
A menial's livery thence to wear !

But sadder yet than all its kind,
The life-long slavery of mind,
When superstition's tyrant-yoke
Remains from day to day unbroke ;
Rules o'er the spirit, makes it toil
To manufacture its own coil—
Build up its prison—lock its cells
And hammer its own manacles ;
Put out its eyes—restrain its feet,
And fix itself to some stone seat ;
Thus chained, imprisoned, tortured, blind—
To glory in a will resigned,
And triumph in its soulless dearth—
The veriest slave in all the earth !

The veriest slave !   Though low his lot,
Even the negro mind can plot
The run for freedom, or the blow
To lay his wife's seducer low ;
Content with liberty to share
The fever's swamp, the wild beast's lair,
And perish, rather than return,
The back to flay, the flesh to burn !
The patriot, too, can bide his time,
And wait till violets are in prime,

Or the wild lapwing's cry is heard,
Or blooms this flower, or sings that bird ;
. And he can whisper, breathing low—
As secret streams through pastures flow,
Bidding the grass-blade to be green,—
His thoughts to others ; till the scene
Around grows brighter, and the rill
That rose first from his lonely hill—
Then secret flowed, with gleamings bright,
Bursts forth a river to the light ;
Then swells a flood—with torrent force,
Breaks down its dams and pours its course
Over the country ; whelming wide
The tyrant's slaves, the oppressor's pride—
Its war of waves, with glorious spray,
Sweeping them from the land away,
And cleansing it from their foul strife
With baptism of arisen life !

Alas ! not thus, with minds who low
To superstition's slavery bow :
They fear to dream of being free,
And dare not plot for liberty ;
They do not own themselves, but give
Their souls to fears which through them live ;

This tyrant creed—that tale of lies,
O'er thought and conscience tyrannize;
They dare not feel—they dare not think;
Bubbles the fount—they dare not drink;
Blossoms the flower—they dare not pluck;
Ripens the fruit—they dare not suck;
Nature is banned to them—they fear
Her form to view, her voice to hear;
Their ears are deaf—their hearts are dull
To all the sweet and beautiful—
Their fears, their foes; themselves, the slaves
Of their own fancies, to their graves;
Than negro worse—than Poland's sons,
Who freedom find in flash of guns;
In superstition's walls confined—
The saddest helots of mankind!

Still change came scenting fresh the air,
And freedom fluted everywhere:
In each new flower, in each bird's song,
Rose, teaching to be sweet and strong;
And when the eve shut pale and dim,
And lost were sounds of vesper hymn,
And every crimson petal's blush
Was burning in the sacred hush—

Opened the gates of garden wall
And quick was heard a firm footfall,
And shadowed in the white moonbeam
A plume o'er gallant head would stream,
And a tall form, with gentle stride,
Move till it reached a fair shape's side :
Then o'er it bend, as bends the pine
Over the larch's softer line ;
The wind of love which ever flows—
Blowing together the dear boughs.

Was it a soldier's form, which high
From the dim shades came towering by ?
Was it the nun's slim shape beside,
And had she lost her pious pride,
And gained the loss by all forgiven,
And risen to love, like lark to heaven ?
So Gerald thought, as leaning o'er
His lattice-sill in twilight hour
He watched those forms together stray,
Then melt into the gloom away ;
So Gerald deemed, and then his mind
Returned to her he had left behind,
Until his musing changed to dream,
And 'mid a tropic summer's beam,

Mounted upon the wings of swallow—
Pursued by thousands with wild hallo—
He seemed to fly, its wings outspanning
Half heaven, with their whirlwind fanning,
And bearing him o'er earth and ocean,
With an orchestra's stormy motion—
When swell the notes yet higher and higher,
And comes the sweetness nigher and nigher,
To ebb and end in gentle fall,
Like a pastoral madrigal,
Where twitter birds and willows quiver
Beside a rimpling English river,
Where Bertha watches swallows glide,
And he is watching at her side.

PART IV.

THE RETURN.

HE dawn is white as bloom of thorn,
 The spurring postman blows his horn—
 A letter with the English mark,
On Gerald's darkness sheds a spark
 Of light and joyousness, for though
He had thrice written, mid the throw
Of things and doings, in his speed
He had forgotten, for her need,
To state the probable address
Would find him from her loveliness;
And, from his fault, her answers thus
Were lost in ways most dolorous;
So swift the marches of his chief,
And bugle call from bivouac brief,

The letters fell behind, or came
In tatters after, lost or lame ;
And then his rest in convent lone,
His place and being kept unknown,
Till consciousness returned, and then
He asked the Sister Nina's pen,
And she wrote for him of his wound
Which long had to his pillow bound,
And added that he trusted quick
To leave the long list of the sick
And homeward tend ; meanwhile requiring
A letter from his love, desiring
To know her welfare : and thus came
Her letter with its answering flame.

O blest the letter that conveys
The hope of years—the joy of days ;
The father's charge, the mother's fears,
Love's welcome, or the trace of tears ;
The well-known hand and customed seal
The fond remembered form reveal,
Which instant shall your thought command,
As rises spring to hazel wand.
A word may join in shine together,
Those who were sundered in cloud weather ;

A few brief lines from friendly hand
Shall bridge the space from land to land,
Bring English scenes to tropic clime,
Put back the minute hand of time,
Show forth once more forgotten places,
Relume again beloved old faces,
Restore the birth-place of your sires,
And groups around its Christmas fires,
Unite the husband to his bride,
Bring severed lovers side by side :
Give hope and cheer from heart to heart,
Though years have passed and seas may part.

To Gerald's ears sweet sung the birds,
While reading Bertha's tender words ;
Brighter the morning sunshine shone,
.The tracery of her thoughts upon ;
All things looked lovelier, as he read
The love which her fond spirit shed,
And how she mourned, yet trusted still
He soon would rise above his ill ;
And how she grieved, and yet hoped ever
No destiny their fates would sever,
But, home returning, love would cast
Still brighter beams from sorrow past,

Upon their hearts, upon their home ;
O welcome day ! O long to come !

No chill rebuke, no word of blame,
Within that loving letter came ;
He had done well to leave his art,
And enter on a nobler part—
To cease to paint and colours dream,
And grow himself some painter's theme.
His wound was sad—she seemed to feel
How painful it had been to heal.
The cruel probe ! she felt it turn
Within the rent, and writhe and burn ;
The savage knife ! she felt its edge ;
The barbarous shell !—its iron wedge ;
Yet had he failed ? his chief had won !
And fallen ? the great deed was done !
And suffered ? Italy was free !—
Free from her mountains to the sea !
And his, with Garibaldi's name,
Wreck-raised would float on sea of fame !

O woman, if to thee were clear
How great thy power to soothe and cheer !

How vast thy influence to arouse
In mind of man the noblest vows !
How strong thy potency to wake
His soul to virtue for thy sake !
Thy will, how mighty to control
The impulse of his striving soul,
And lead him from the lower things
To soar upon aspiring wings,
And from the paths of vain pretence
To scale the heights of excellence !
Thou wouldst not be content to fall
To his poor plaything or his thrall ;
But keep the station to thee given,
And move by man his guide to heaven—
His inspiration through earth's strife—
His angel of the higher life !

" Come home," wrote Bertha ; " welcome there !
Thy form though marred—thy wounds are fair !
Come home—thy home is by my side ;
Thy home within my heart is wide.
Thou wilt come home, and fill its gate
With joy, and love shall on thee wait ;
Thou wilt come home, and all be well,
So will my hopes prophetic tell ;

Thou wilt come home, and bring with thee
Treasure more rich than art could be—
The sense of suffering for the right—
The scar gained in a noble fight !
And though the limb may limp, thy state
Be Jacob-like, who strove with fate,
Wrestling with it till break of day—
Bearing its blessing then away :
And though thou stoop'st, I will not call
Thee else than poplar, straight and tall,
For thou hast done the act thy hand
Didst find to do, with gallant brand ;
And made thy thought and life agree,
And helped a land to liberty !"

"Come home," wrote Bertha ; "soon the bird
Should herald thee, will now be heard !
I keep thy pledge within my soul—
The season comes to make it whole !
Soon to these cold, yet well-loved skies,
On annual round the swallow flies ;
Soon will its purpled silver gleam
Amid the waters of our stream—
Soon will its twitter music make—
A song beloved for thy sake !

Soon will its curving flight awaken
Thoughts of its longer circuit taken ;
Then with that gentle swallow come,
Back to thy Bertha and thy home.
For with the swallow, summer hours
And sunny skies and blosmy flowers,
And growing corn, and shining leaves,
And river walks, and happy eves,
And woodland song and insect hum
Will, dearest, with thy promise come ;
For in the truth that I have trusted,
Are all sweet things and fair adjusted ;
I much should do thee wrong to doubt thee,
But sad the river-walk without thee.
Then, Gerald, come ! Come home ! come home !
Come, with that gentle swallow, come !"

He read the letter through and through,
And wings within his spirit grew.
How could he keep from her, who cried
Thus sweetly for him by her side ?
Her words were music to his soul,
And motion to his spirit stole,
As dance comes to the feet, when viol
Speaks and forbids all faint denial.

Yet was he wan, and weak, and lame,
And would she be to him the same?
O yes, she would! Why should he fear
Her form to see, her voice to hear?—
That form, whose semblance ne'er would part
From the bright mirror of his heart—
That voice, which on his spirit's ear
Came like sweet sounds from highest sphere,
When listening earth, with thirsty mouth,
Quaffs the rich rain-drops of the south.

A purple eve, a golden morn,
Died in the west, in east was born;
Yet ere the day was well begun,
And paled the stars before the sun,
A carriage drove up to the gate,
Nor had the bright steeds long to wait.
Quick Gerald entered, and espied
Another carriage by his side;
That form within it, straight and tall,
His memory could sure recall;
Another shape, of outline thin,
With manly warmth it welcomed in;
A blushing cheek, a graceful wave,
Were all the farewell that she gave;

They told her tale—that she had found
A freedom in which two were bound.
Then saw he Sister Nina last—
Her fair face paling in the past,
As swiftly spurred, from those walls grey,
Galloped the steeds their varied way.

O, soon, how dear becomes a place
Where we have halted in life's race,
Where we have sheltered from strife's din,
And from life's storms found peace within !
That convent lone—those grey stone walls
With lichen stained, and dark moss-balls ;
That little cell, that ivied bank,
That fountain worn, that garden dank,
That gateway quaint, whence he had past,
In Gerald's memory long would last,
Like shrine where travellers stop for prayer,
And find some sacred moments there.

Who has not seen, when journeying through
A clouded land, a speck of blue ?
Who has not gained, when travelling on,
A glimpse of that too quickly gone ?

Who has not on life's pathways met
A form which he could ne'er forget?
Which rose upon him suddenly,
Then faded, as 'twere not to be,
Which swiftly flashed on him its light,
Then passed as swiftly from his sight;
As Nina's form o'er Gerald came,
A pale, yet an enchanting flame—
A vision white as fountain's gush,
Which love's flower lent a transient blush,
Quick silvering to its crystal sphere—
Its music but for listening ear—
Its purity, a passing gleam
Of heaven's light, for memory's dream.

Speed, horses, speed; the shore is won,
The sea is gained, the sail begun!
Fly, vessel, fly; delay is drear,
The land looms large, the port is here!
Yet what tired flutterer o'er the deep
Does there aloft its watches keep,
With sleeky plumes and sleepy eye,
And beak its little bosom by?
Reef gently, gentle mariner,
For it is summer's harbinger—

Tired, like thee, of sea and sky,
And longing to green fields to fly !
The pulley creaks, it upward springs,
And landward flies with circling wings.

Loud rings the bell, the train is due,
The shrieking engine steams in view,
Then puffing, snorting, forward dashes,
Through cut and tunnel onward flashes,
By gold-broomed bank and wooded sides,
O'er bridge, where river under glides,
Through park, where cattle browsing stray,
Through smoky town and village gay,
By verdant mead and springing wheat,
By cottage thatched and terraced seat,
By rising mound, with hyacinths blue,
By ferny nooks, which tressy grew,
O'er spreading plain, through tunnelled hill,
Past ruined tower, past wind-swept mill,
Past chimneys tall, and red forge fires,
Black grimy pits, white village spires,
Green England blooming in its pride—
The long steam-banner floating wide !

Home, home; yes, home! the dearest spot!
Heaven's nook on earth! earth's angel lot!
The dear old place again appears,
Its long familiar form it wears!
There, o'er the trees, the grey church tower
Reminds of many a sacred hour!
There the green lane winds onward still!
There the white path climbs o'er the hill!
There flows the river through the woods!
There are the old ancestral roods!
And there two houses, close together,
Basking amid the shining weather—
The home where Gerald first breath drew—
The home where Bertha beauteous grew!

That eve the rippling river, sweet,
Sung welcome to their truant feet—
Once more along its banks they strayed—
Once more its foam-bells music played—
Again they saw its grasses gleam
In emerald, 'mid its crystal stream;
Again they viewed the hanging wood,
Downward reflected in the flood;
Again beneath one tree they pledge
Their troth to life's remotest edge;

While past a swallow wheels in flight
Its shining wings and body bright,
And both looked upward to the skies,
Then melted in each other's eyes.

" Is it," said he, " that bird of mine,
Which that sad eve became our sign ?
'Twere strange, if so ! yet all is strange,
And order sweet rules o'er our change."
And then he told, as in a tale,
Of the tired flutterer on the sail—
How dim its little rounded eye !
How on its breast its beak would lie !
How frayed its plumes ! how dull their light !
And of its weak and frightened flight.

" It is that bird," she cried ; " I know,
For o'er my soul it cast a glow—
A sense of something felt before,
Which shed a warmth my spirit o'er !
Among ten thousand of its kind
That blessed bird I sure should find.
My faith is strong in it and Him
Who bore it from the ocean's rim,

Who brought you safe through battle's strife,
And kept for me your loving life !
It is our bird—the wanderer wide
You chose for sign, and pledge, and guide,
Whom powers prophetic have proved true—
Who brings my summer bringing you,
Whose circling wings our love should earn—
The bird of promise and return !"

Gerald replied, " Dear maid, thy faith
Is kin to that which conquers death—
'Tis that which bids its wish, become—
'Tis that sweet faith has brought me home.
Yet would I doubt not thy belief
In that bright bird, though proof be brief—
All motion is by one breath stirred—
Who grants the prophet, sends the bird !
Then hence on gold o'er shield or urn
One swallow shall in purple burn—
Our blazoned scutcheon, while its race
We choose henceforth our faith to grace,
And raise it, as on circling wings,
While linnet flies or mavis sings.
To comfort us when winter lours,
We know the swallow will bring flowers ;

When earth is dark and skies are drear
Its chirp shall come on memory's ear,
Herald to earth of warmth and bloom,
Bringer of brightness and perfume,
The harbinger of sunset eves,
The prophet of ripe amber sheaves :
Unto our children it shall teach
The holiest truths the heavens preach ;
The faith in better days for earth—
The summer of a heavenly birth—
The promise of a longer day,
When all time's woes shall pass away !
And when in wanderings they discern
Its radiant wings, they home shall turn ;
And learn from it the lesson blest,
To seek again the parent nest :
From foreign lands and strife to come,
And love their country and their home."

Ring, marriage bells, the blissful hour,
Shake to its base the old church tower !
Ring, marriage bells, the happy pair,
Cast forth your joy-peals o'er the air,
Fling wide your storm of joyful sound,
Valley and hill and stream around,

Till every bird joins in the note,
And strains with joy its tender throat,
And the sweet river ever glides,
Made musicaler by your tides!
Ring, marriage bells! my tale is done,
Its teller blest, if only one,
Rises up better, stronger, sweeter—
In aught of thought or will completer—
From what is rhymed of love and faith,
Of nature's scenes, of patriot's death,
Of war for right, of duty felt,
Of daring brave, of good blows dealt,
Of vow performed, of troth maintained,
Of love increased, of welcome gained,
Of sunshine coming after gloom,
Of love of country and of home,
And that bright bird, whose circling flight
Gleams through my song and gives it light!

THE SCENES OF SPRING.

F

The Scenes of Spring.

I.

GOD of the years, and of the seasons Lord !
Changeless in change ; by progress best adored ;
Time to eternity thy praise accord !

Thy new year comes, and with it flows the song,
As from the radiant Ram the young sun, strong,
Through heaven's plains trails the gold fleece along ;

While spreads forth with the skiey eastern glow—
A breath, an air, a palpitating flow
Of warmth, in sparkles bathing all below.

All has fresh life beneath the sun's bright eye :
Broader the blue above, more clear the sky,
Less shadowy earth and greener ocean's dye.

There comes a warm fond breath upon the cheek :
A warmth within of which words poorly speak :
A warmth yet eloquent as the flower's red streak.

Welcome, ye scenes of Spring ! before me rise
Your gladdening green—the blueness of your skies :
Symbols of youth and types of Paradise !

II.

O COME, fair Spring ! with spirit warm and genial
Unto my heart's core, and O deem it venial
That I solicit thee with no thoughts menial.

I am not thine, but thou art mine for ever,
So I can clasp thee to my heart, nor sever
Thy warmth from me, so that my soul fail never.

For state of soul makes its own state of season ;
And wintry souls are proven in high treason
To the soul's sceptre and right royal reason.

If calm within, who heeds the storm's vain bicker ?
And widest does the soul's bright taper flicker,
When black eclipse makes night's dun darkness thicker.

My Spring thou art, if I with thee am vernal ;
As up amid the spirit spheres supernal,
Thy rising song is floating for the Eternal !

Yet not for me, O Spring ! perpetual pleasure ;
O, not for me, the balanced step of leisure ;
O, not for me, the abiding stores of treasure ;—

The steadfast state—the indomitable spirit ;
The rock-like power—the constant meed of merit,
In changing planet how can man inherit ?

Still of myself, O Spring, I take thy teaching ;
Within my soul that high endeavour reaching,
Which thou art ever in some new form preaching.

My handmaid thou, with downy cheeklets flushing,
To hand me blossoms all bedewed and blushing,
With all sweet words as from morn's songsters gushing.

And these will teach with lessons ever kind,
The outer sphere with inner state to bind,
And show how Nature ministers to Mind.

III.

THY bugle, March! is ringing loud and clear ;
Thy high tempestuous tones of wrath I hear ;
Driving through heaven, thou wild young charioteer !

Thy chariot flashes on, and naught impedes
Its circling course, through the sky's azure meads,
Star-wheeled, cloud-compassed and with aëry steeds.

Fed upon wind, in winged strength they fly ;
Their proud necks arching, maned with mists on high,
And hoofs fire-striking, through the gusty sky.

Meanwhile thy bugle-blasts more loudly sound,
Each blast the dark clouds scattering around,
And wakening wintry sleepers underground.

They wake, they rise, and come forth in their courses,
As though an angel touched anew life's sources,
And the ground gaped and Death gave up his forces.

IV.

Thou too, fair April, with thy moistened locks,
And sunny eye-beam which a dew-drop mocks;
Sitting like shepherdess amid her flocks:

The clouds, thy flocks; O press their fleeces dry!
Bright rains descend, like tears from thine own eye,
And laughs and weeps the variable sky.

Thou pressest the fair clouds which round thee muster,
As vintager may press the grape's sweet cluster,
And then the sunny sky laughs out in lustre.

The earth preserves the tears Heaven sheds for thee,
With pious care; and 'neath yon rooty tree
The red-brown mosses soon in green shall be.

The young seed shoots, and unto it is given—
Its old husk shed and its new being shriven—
The brightest baptism of rain from heaven.

v.

COME, with slim foot which scarce the dew-drop brushes,
Thy cheeks, O May, covered with eastern blushes,
Thy head flower-decked amid a braid of rushes.

Press but thy foot, and there upsprings the daisy ;
Breathe, and at once dissolve all mist-wreaths hazy ;
Move, and the young leaves dance in measures mazy.

Thy blue eye gives the violet its hue,
Thy red cheeks blush the hawthorn blossoms through,
Thy golden locks, laburnum-tressed, we view !

From thy fair fingers drop all fairest flowers,
Starry and coronal, with honied dowers,
Or cupped, or belled, or mouthed, of gifted powers :

Or chequered—streaked, or with rich blotches dyed ;
Or pencilled daintily, or quaintly pied—
The field's, the forest's, and the garden's pride !

To thee, Enchantress, all these charms we owe ;
As o'er bare canvas bends the artist's brow,
And lights are shed, and glorious colours glow.

To thee, O month of flowers, we owe the sight
Of kingcups rich and spangling paigles bright,
The earth's true gold—her purest wealth of light :

Each bud, a mouth to speak of God's creation—
Each bloom, a smile of Love's own consecration—
All flowers, earth's laughter and joy's revelation !

VI.

ONCE, in the vision of a wintry eve,
The spirit's eye a picture bright would weave
Of children three, which came and would not leave.

The one : a boy of dark eye and brow fair ;
Who rushed past, swift as meteor in the air,
While the wild winds were toying with his hair.

The next : a delicate and graceful girl ;
As in sweet sorrow, moistened each bright curl ;
Sunnily smiling ; in each eye a pearl.

The last : a little laughing blushing maiden,
Blooming as flower or like a rainbow braiden,
Like flower with sweets, like bow with sunshine laden.

Distinct each one—yet each a lovely thing ;
Of the three-chorded lute, to each a string :
So lovely each, the three months of the Spring.

VII.

THERE are winged glories in the meanest midge ;
And April wends to May o'er skiey ridge,
Or o'er the arch of the bright rainbow's bridge.

And so, my song, mayst thou take wings, and fly,
And scale the highest heart through brightest eye,
Until absorbed in the starry Harp on high.

And thus, my song, ascend—ascend, and bear
A brighter Spring to bosoms nipped with care ;
And bridge the soul, as with hope's rainbow fair.

Through April showers of sympathy we glide,
To May's delight and efflorescent pride :
As swell the waters to the full spring tide.

Through winds of March the air of May is warm,
And clear the sky shines from the expended storm :
As all things join each other's weal to form.

VIII.

Lo, Spring is on the waters! and emotion,
At its approach, swells o'er the briny ocean,
And makes its bosom surge with fond commotion.

The headland climb; look o'er the watery scene!
Mark in the sun the waves how emerald green!
See how they break in lines of crested sheen!

Up in the morning; watch the fishes glide
In silvery shoals, by young fins multiplied:
Their sparkling scales bright gleaming through the tide.

Linger at eve; and see the bright sun-set,
No more amid a wide cloud-rack of jet,
But in a west more clear and yellower yet.

Swift rise the waters; swift the spring tides o'er
The fisher's threshold and his rush-strewn floor,
Pour moon-moved currents, and swift leave the shore.

Such things are seen ; O for the high emprise
And diver's strength, to open wide the eyes
Where in the deep are wave-whelmed argosies.

Where round the brazen beaks of galleys old,
The sea-weed greener spreads its tangled hold,
And young whales game o'er untold Spanish gold.

Where the shell's trumpet twirl, or purple lip,
May aye be sounded, or may ever sip ;
There, valour's shoulder blade—there, beauty's hip !

O for the eyes to see the quaint procession,
With which Spring openeth her ocean session,
Charging the waves to ever new progression.

Leviathan shall then the sea snakes muster ;
The unknown monsters of the great deeps cluster,
And ocean's sparry halls remit new lustre.

The branchy coral bowers glow rosier then ;
The mermaids give some bosom thoughts to men ;
And those bleached bones dream they shall knit again.

IX.

Down in the earth descend, and Spring is there ;
Upturn the mould, and scent her breath so rare ;
See how it steams, inspired with ardour fair !

Down 'mid the clods, with the good farmer mole,
Or with the eyeless worm send forth thy soul,
Call no part mean, for God has made the whole.

Behold the ant amid her long white eggs,
Raising her mound firm, without piles or pegs—
The quickened motion of those hundred legs ;

The dewy grub, of nightingales the food ;
The reddening fibres from the neighbouring wood ;
The rising sap—and say, that all is good !

Seest thou the seeds with subterranean eyes !
Each little germ drains moisture from the skies :
It quickens, swells, and, lo, its sprouts arise !

O seeds of soul, like seeds amid the ground,
Not in the outward-shown existence found ;
As they were once, ye are by fast frosts bound !

How silently they lay !   Not many know
That ye, awakened, in the breast may glow,
And moral Spring yet bid ye bud and blow.

As seeds in earth, so souls amid the ages,
Have germs of heroes, prophets, saints and sages ;
And many yet shall fill life's brightest pages.

That mealy grub let no vain thought despise ;
To-morrow, winged, it shall have circled eyes,
Chequers and bars of gold and crimson dyes.

Its new and higher life shall be begun,
Its wings shall spread the painted air upon,
And flash a flying blossom in the sun.

X.

SPRING in the woods! The sap is rising fast,
Each trunk would add a new ring to the last,
To note a fresh Spring come—a winter past.

Clearer the bark becomes; the branches bud,
Hang forth fair tassels, or their twigs red stud;
Such strength is coursing through their young green
    blood.

The pale sprouts swell, in close wrapped sheaths con-
    fined:
Spread their curled leaves, for rain, and sun, and wind,
And full burst, cast their gummy swathes behind.

Then scarce-seen blossoms lightly hued and thin,
Or bunched, or tasselled, drop with slightest din,
And strew the grass the trees' broad shade within.

G

And closely watched—the acorn cup, behold !
The beech-nut's husk ; the filbert brown, foretold ;
And smallest purple cones on fir tree old.

So sweet, so fresh—the leafiness of Spring,
The flowers must blossom, and the birds must sing,
And Hope flush red, and Love have buoyant wing.

The dry, sere, yellow leaves of sin and sorrow,
Who would not cast from his soul's trunk to-morrow,
And from the woods of Spring a lesson borrow ?

With Spring's green leaves unfolding o'er the glade,
By Love and Charity O be there made
A freshening verdure and a sheltering shade !

XI.

Spring with the birds ! The wild swan has gone forth
With swarming smews, as at its coming wroth,
Back to the snows of their own native north.

So wintry souls their manners cold prefer,
And from the rising warmth suspicious stir ;
While the ringed turtle is Spring's harbinger.

How plaintive, sweet, and fond, its gentle coo !
The strength of all love's whispers to and fro
Flows on the ear, with all love's joy and woe.

The sparrow chirpeth of green buds and leaves ;
The tom-tit hangs upon the barn's thatched eaves ;
And corn-crakes dream of burnished golden sheaves.

Red-breasted robin, chill and silent long,
Now greets the garden sunshine with a song ;
Let no cold thought its warm-hued bosom wrong.

Hark! in the copse the ruby pheasant's crow,
Amid the boughs which spray us as we go;
And hist! it flits past like a transient glow.

The small grey linnet sings like tinkling rill;
Its green-plumed sister has no tuneful bill;
Thus just is God in compensations still!

The blackbird pipes amid the nutty buds;
The thrush, the air with shower of music floods;
Songful the hedge-rows green, the fields, the woods.

Skimming the stream, the swallow's twittering throat
Of other lands and travels far has note,
And tells of tales all marvellous and unwrote.

Afar we hear the cuckoo's echoing cry
Called through the air, in clear monotony;
One Voice of many where no Life we spy.

By wildest tarn, most solitary mere,
Fly feathery forms, new moulted plumes appear;
No nook from whence no tuneful throats we hear.

Most glorious songs, that from the human heart
Swell forth your strains, thus birds reveal your part !
God loves the poet—sacred is his art !

O that, awoke by vernal songster's strain
Man moved to Music ; then no war-red plain,
But universal harmony should reign.

XII.

MOULT with the birds, ye red-cloaked warriors! change
Your blood-stained raiment, and o'er ploughed fields
    range,
And man no more from brother-man estrange.

Ye souls, so covetous of corn and herds,
Whose jaundiced eyes would turn life's cream to curds;
Doff miser robes, and moult ye with the birds.

Moult with the birds, ye lawyers with long curls!
Leave to the moth your Chancery twists and twirls;
Off gown and wig! No swine require your pearls.

Ye minds all ignorant, and dark, and drear,
As owlet's eyes at sunrise, blank and blear;
Moult with day's birds, and let the light appear.

Moult with the birds, ye black-robed priests ! and wear
Saint's robes of radiance, and the truth declare
That bids us hope in God and not despair.

Ye tongues, so blistered with deceiving words !
Ye slaves, whip-goaded like dumb, driven herds !
There's Spring for all ; then moult ye with the birds.

Off, feathers frayed and faded, coarse and blurred ;
On, glossy plumes, and let sweet songs be heard !
Through pain comes pleasure, and so moults the bird.

XIII.

Spring, thou art love as well as loveliness,
And song and gladness; and the heart's distress
Thou comest to soothe, heal, recompense, and bless.

God's love thou showest in thy smiling face—
The soft, sweet, shining, brightening of His grace;
The glory raying from His high dwelling-place.

Love's season art thou; nothing would be single;
All Nature's pulses warmer burn and tingle,
And flush with flush and beam with beam commingle.

Each opening blossom feels the soft desire,
And to each neighbouring blossom drawing nigher,
Gives golden joy that fills its cup with fire.

The little birds indulge love's wayward flight,
Then sidle near, and swift their wings excite,
While each fine feather quivers with delight.

And man ? shall he not feel the power of Spring,
To burnish love's plumes, and to prune its wing,
And bid it sweeter, softer wood-notes sing ?

Yet higher love, O Spring, thy sunshine bringeth,
Than ring-dove cooeth or than goldfinch singeth—
A love of richer peals than blue bell ringeth.

With fresher flowers the poet wreaths his locks,
And shepherds with new oaten pipe his flocks ;
Inspired once more to dream of golden shocks.

His voice is clearer ; more he loves his art ;
And kindlier fancies through his brain-nerves start ;
Then move his tongue, and thrill through every heart.

Their country's love, the patriots warmer feel,
By all its beauty ; and its wounds would heal,
With all the warmth which fires the common weal.

And Thou, O God ! the soul with passion gloweth,
In Spring's fair season which Thy love bestoweth,
For Thee, and Thy dear joy, which downward floweth.

It waits, it pants, it thrills with soft desire,
To feel Thy fulness, to drink in Thy fire ;
That Thou with it should dwell, for ever nigher—
    nigher !

XIV.

GIVE thanks to Him, whose steadfast laws ordain
Seed-time and harvest, ever should remain ;
Bless Him, ye seasons, for His loving reign.

And thou, O Spring ! worship Him with thy daisies—
Eyes turned to heaven ; and sing His heartfelt praises,
From all thy tuneful throats in woodland mazes.

Wondrous His work, when with invisible hand
He scatters countless seeds throughout the land,
And birds and breezes serve His wide command.

Wondrous His work, when, in the womb of earth,
Spring quickeneth the little germs to birth,
And acorns swell.to reach the old oak's girth.

O Father—God, who, owning Nature—wife,
Createst beauty out of the sweet strife ;
Art seed of seeds, and very Life of Life ;

Spring praises Thee throughout her generations;
Tells of Thy goodness in her vegetations;
Blooms to Thy glory through her flowery nations.

The germinating seed; the budding tree;
The shoot—the sprout—the swelling spirit's key;
The quickening life, O Father, speak of Thee.

XV.

PLOUGHMAN, a-field ! the dewy morn is fair,
Yet still thy breath is wreathed upon the air ;
Harness the team, and fix the shining share.

Now guide the coulter, and, with even sight,
Force deep the share, and cut the furrow straight,
And turn each black ridge side-ways to the right.

So he who drives the white Parnassian teams,
Pages of rag with glorious work redeems ;
Each placed aside, till filled the radiant reams.

Alike as labourers do the Fates regard
Peasant and ploughman, patriot and bard—
The painter's small palm and the hind's hand hard.

Ye men of tillage, and ye men who write ;
For each one common cause—one duty bright ;
Two close-clasped hands, whose union is might.

Producers both, your different spheres ye find :
To till the soil, to cultivate the mind,
Direct the heart, and train the strong and kind.

Holy your labours—unto virtue sealed ;
God worketh yet ; in works, His word revealed ;
What incense rises from the fresh-ploughed field !

Healthy the steam from every new-turned clod ;
Sweet also work to turn the soul to God ;
All skiey glories rise from earth's poor sod.

Patient the rook pursues the upturning share,
The red worm gaining for his thrifty care ;
So speed the plough, that all may have and spare.

Hands to the plough ! whoever turneth back
Is not fit workman !   By that cloudy rack,
Let man work on—the Heavens are not slack !

Plough down the hill that's stained with human blood,
Plough the wide plain of human brotherhood ;
Plough freedom's fields—the rich glebes of the good.

Plough o'er the palaces of tyrant pride,
And o'er false temples let the bright share glide ;
As o'er doomed cities old, spread ruin wide.

To fit the field to take the wondrous seed,
To move the brain its thronging thoughts to breed :
Such ploughman's labour, and such patriot's deed.

How wide the uncultured acres spread, and, lo !
How vast the ignorance, the want, the woe ;
So speed the plough—there's mighty work to do.

XVI.

Sower, go forth! and with well-measured stride,
And balanced body, swung from side to side,
Spread forth thy hand and cast thy treasure wide.

From the coarse bag athwart thy stout breast hung,
Draw forth thy golden seed, which broad-cast flung,
Shall yet arise the binding weed among.

Though poppies redden, purple thistles rear,
And knotted grasses point the verdurous spear;
Sow step by step—thy harvest shall appear.

Let the rough harrow close thy useful toil,
Or the drill's labour, and the scattered soil
The roller press, for the rich autumn spoil.

So, sower of the Word! pass o'er the land,
Sowing thy seed : no longer idly stand ;
Sow in the morn, nor let eve stay thy hand.

Beside all waters sow, though jointed weed
Or choking creeper struggle with thy deed ;
Thou hast thy labour done and earned thy meed.

Though tangling briar upon thy borders press,
Labour shall prune the world's rough wilderness,
And blooming roses its wide desert bless.

The glance of goodness to the heart shall come ;
Nor word, nor tract, fall seedless into gloom :
And spring-tide sowing have its harvest home.

XVII.

A MOTHER sweet, a mother dear, is Spring;
Calling her children round her in a ring,
Like One who sat once on the purple ling.

All motherly she is; with sweet surmise,
Watching the little sleeper's closen eyes,
Till bright blue buds from leaf-like lids they rise.

And sweet her breath as mother's, when neck bare
She lieth by her sleeping infant fair;
And the dear child is conscious she is there.

And O, she cometh over us with sense
Of so much love and such fond providence,
We reach to her arms in fearless confidence.

We lap our lives in hers, and revelling roll
With limb-like nakedness of joyous soul,
And feel the gain of yielding to the full.

Her looks all childhood's sweet thoughts to us bring ;
Into her nestling arms our lives we fling :
A mother sweet—a mother dear, is Spring.

XVIII.

DIDST ever see the children of the Spring?
The gold, grey gnat, with gleam of glancing wing,
The new-born flies afloat, in mazy ring.

Didst ever see, within the greenwood free,
The young deer feeding, at your footfall flee;
Or lambkins frisking o'er the daisied lea?

Didst ever see the feathered flutterer strive
To leave its nest; or from the yellow hive
The brown swarm buzzing on the bright breeze drive?

Didst ever see the patient partridge lead
Its short-tailed brood amid the furrowed seed;
Or water chicks to sedgy streamlets speed?

Didst ever see the young field-mouse, with eye
So black and quick; the old lark from the sky
Drop o'er its nest; the startled leveret fly?

Didst ever see the mushroom's fairy ring—
The budding bloom—the butterfly's bright wing？
Fair family, these—all children of the Spring！

XIX.

STEP to the orchard !   Blushing through the breeze,
What lovely cheeks of clustering blossoms these—
That tint the air around our apple trees !

Bright births of Beauty's fair and rosy races :
In all the innocence of childlike graces,
Peer forth the sweet hues of their delicate faces !

With sweetening smiles, they are together wreathing ;
' With laughing looks, they are the breeze back breathing;
Hue to the air, and scent to breeze bequeathing ;

While, idyl sweet ! flower-laden branches swaying,
Shower their bright petals o'er the children playing :
Their long locks fair, with beauteous bloom arraying ;

And round the tree-trunks, silvery and sage,
Drift fallen blossoms, giving tender gage
That youthful thoughts most kindly nourish age.

XX.

WALK to the meads! How sweetly for the eye,
Slant to the sun, those upland meadows lie ;
Where those white lambkins gleely frisk on high.

And see how lush the lowland grass has sprung,
Spangled with daisies, gold kingcups among—
Long purples, crowfoot, and the bluehound's tongue.

And thou, O happy, happy, milk-white steer ;
Beside those low thatched homesteads feeding there,
Rejoice ! for thee at least no altar bier—

No sacrificing priest, no flower-decked death,
No choral hymn that last groan covereth :
Thy flanks' fair beauty fatal to thy breath.

Joy while thou mayest; wouldst thou had naught to
     dare,
No other knife bright gleaming through the air;
Go, join thy fellows 'neath those elm-trees fair!

Chewing the cud, with a reflective grace,
And mild deep quietude in each fine face;
Their dark eyes roll, their red flanks paint the place.

Their switching tails the sparkling flies disturb,
Their broad necks undulate with swell superb,
Their large white teeth gleam 'mid the sweet green
     herb.

Their fragrant breaths mix with the fume of flowers,
And smell of grass-blooms, and their leafy bowers
Blend with the mead's green—stretching to the moors.

XXI.

THROUGH the field paths ! Behold the country wide,
Mapped out with hedges ; each division dyed
With varied green, and soil diversified.

There the rich glebe, so red, would seem to bloom ;
And there are claylands white, and now we roam
Through the blue marl and the deep yellow loam.

There the young turnips spread their earliest green,
And there the ground the soft-hued wheat blades screen,
That red-veined mangel and rathe vetch between.

To those tall poles, attached with tender twine,
Cling the young hop plants, with their juicy bine,
As to the elm trees cling the loving vine.

And see, the breeze breathes o'er those barley blades,
And wave on wave of verdure shines and fades,
Flowing in all diversity of shades.

XXII.

O THANKS, O thanks! the ploughman has his meed;
The sower not in vain has cast his seed;
There is no thought, but springeth up in deed.

Within the mossy home of true love's nest,
Grouped glittering globes—five shining blue eggs rest;
And look again! five flutterers feathery drest!

Beneath the earth the little seed was bound:
Bright insects, sing! it has risen from the ground:
Dance to its shade! it greens the country round.

Thanks, too, O Man, from thee: for Spring has given
That which it promised thee, a little leaven
For thy life's lump, from out a bluer heaven.

Around, a greener earth; above, a sky
More sunny bright; beneath, less shadows lie;
Then, thank thou GOD—more glorious far on high!

XXIII.

Pass o'er our hearts, O Spring, and let thy breath
Sweeten our lives ; as the old legend saith,
The rose perfumes its soil, though heaped o'er death.

Pass o'er our hearts, our dormant spirits quicken
Unto strong birth ; no more to pale and sicken,
But dare and do, where most life's combats thicken.

Pass o'er our hearts, and let the sprouts of spirit,
Whose germs from God's own goodness we inherit,
Spread forth and branch in budding boughs of merit.

Buds of true beauty, open in the mind ;
Flowers of affection, be with heart-strings twined ;
Garlands of blossom, on our life's brows bind !

Let tell-tale birds within our bosoms warble,
That life is neither gloss of beauteous bauble,
Nor wears strange mask of some old Gothic corbel.

Let all the voices of the Spring declare,
How psalms of duty raise life's pleasant air,
To hallelujah notes from heaven's choir fair.

And let this warm breath, and these beauteous flowers,
And these sweet songs, endow these hearts of ours
With growth, and bliss, of inward verdant hours.

With youthful energy strike every string;
A vernal virtue to our bosoms bring;
In moral strength pass o'er our hearts, O Spring!

XXIV.

In thy bright might pass through the nations, Spring !
On the broad pinions of fair Freedom's wing :
Arise and shine, that earth's cold statues sing !

Waken the sleepers in sad comfort curled ;
Shout, loudly shout ! hold Freedom's flag unfurled ;
And rouse the slothful nations of the world !

The Lands shall hear thee, and the bounding ocean
Bear thy commands abroad, in fond devotion :
Its waves surged high to hail the glad commotion.

The Lands lie sleeping ; o'er the waves the sun
In more than regal crimson bursts upon
Their wintry sloth, and, lo, their Spring's begun !

Italy wakens, and her unclosed eyes
Match soon the sapphire of her cloudless skies ;
The Seven Hills shout ! again, Rome's eagle flies !

From Poland's sepulchre, a hollow sound;
The marble rends—upheaves; and, with a bound,
A youth, deemed dead, claims his ancestral ground.

Hungaria rises, and, from her warm eye,
Back to the north the chilling snow-storms fly,
And vernal wheat-blades gladden far the sky.

And thou, O Greece, re-echoest thy pæan,
O'er shining waves of thy most blue Ægean;
Thy Delphi sings, and blooms thy vale Tempean.

From sea to sea, from stretching strand to strand,
The vernal sunrise lights, with kindling wand,
And freedom's fires glance bright from land to land.

Shine, Sun of Spring, far o'er the nations shine;
Dispel their darkness—show thy saving sign,
And the world waken with thy light divine.

XXV.

HEAVEN dawneth like thee, Spring! O holy truth!
Grey locks of age to golden curls of youth
Shall change, with scowl of ire to smile of ruth.

The night of time and space shall pass away ;
The winter of the grave shall yield its sway ;
And vernal wings shall shine in morning ray.

Upon the winter of the world shall burst
Another Spring—a second Spring : the thirst
For which shall drain each fountain of the first.

Our first-loved Spring—the Spring the bard has sung,
Shall pass away, the haunts of earth among,
And rise in homes of Heaven for ever young.

Rich raiment with each whimpling crease estranged ;
Beauty to Blessed Beauty shall be changed ;
Each line of loveliness more fair arranged.

Fresh flowers—new odours, shall exhale and rise ;
New notes be sung, and coloured choicer dyes ;
On nightless earths, beneath far rosier skies.

All shall be youth, all morning, and all Spring ;
And each fair wind that woos a thrilling string,
The Spring of Heaven in angel verse shall sing.

That Heavenly Spring, for ever, ever dear,
Saved spirits chant from starry sphere to sphere,
Lay hand on heart, and shout—'tis here, 'tis here !

Thus when the maiden, beautiful on earth,
Awakes in Heaven in a more beauteous birth,
Celestial choirs resound with holy mirth.

The harps of Heaven their sacred preludes play,
The golden crowns take lustre from the day,
And of the Glory brighter beams each ray.

POEMS.

Poems.

THE STREAM OF TIME.

ONWARD flows the Stream of Time,
　　Wave on wave, with course sublime—
　　　Rippling, bubbling, gurgling ; roaming,
　　Babbling, tinkling, singing on ;
　　Rising, spreading, flooding, foaming,
　　　Surging, billowing, ebbing—gone !
Now with gentle purling playing
　　O'er the pebbles of the rill ;
Now with quiet motion straying
O'er bright sands, so blue and still ;
Now with gurgling dimples ringing
　　Foam-bells, lily-like and fair ;

Now like mermaid sweetly singing,
  Parting trim the rushes' hair;
Or adown the mountain dashing,
  Wreathing rainbows in the sun;
Streaming, beaming, sparkling, flashing,
  Tumbling, falling, leaping, rushing,
Booming, foaming—echoing—crushing,
  Crowned with spray-clouds, thunders on.

Onward flows the Stream of Time,
  From the dim eternal mountains,
With a distant echoing chime,
  Rising from their sun-like fountains;
Onward—from those streams which bounded
  Eden's garden's golden prime,
And each breast of green earth rounded,
  In that paradise of time,
Where the voice of God first sounded
  In the sweet Arcadian clime,
And the world's great pulse was founded
  Upon harmony and rhyme.

With bright trains of mist attended,
  On still flows the Stream of Time,

In the depth of ages splendid
  As a distant torrent's chime ;
Through the dark primæval wild wood,
  Far from Eden's flowers it rushes ;
With the eagle's mighty childhood
  From the mountain tarn it gushes ;
Like a snake it hath unrolled
Its treacherous folds of blue and gold ;
Like a long gaunt wolf it speedeth
  Through the hide-clad shepherd's flock,
Flooding where the white lamb feedeth,
  Gulphing vale and scaling rock ;
But amid the pastures still,
  Sometimes flowing sweet in glee,
Like a gently-tinkling rill
  Playing rural minstrelsy :
Well accompanied by the reed
  Damon plays to lover's gushes,
While the lambs beside him feed,
  And the willing Phillis blushes—
Willing nymph and loving swain !
Notes of that old pastoral strain !

Onward flows the Stream of Time—
  Past the shepherd's pasture fair,

Down to where the spreading lime
    Shades the tribe's huts circled there ;
Where, beside the beaver's dyke,
    Swarthy clans have built their homes,
Who in moonlight's white beam strike
    The yellow salmon as it roams ;
Or in noontide's scorching hour
    Lave their limbs amid its stream ;
Bind the bark and try its power
    O'er the swelling waves to gleam ;
Or beside its leafy bank,
    Hunt wild Nature's savage brood,
In the trackless forest dank,
    Dreadful in its solitude,
    Lonely in its sweetest mood,
As they pass its rocks sublime,
Sailing on the Stream of Time.

On it flows : its many waves
    Gushing, eddying, roaring on,
Past the tribesmen's mounded graves,
    'Neath the setting of the sun ;
On to where the great chief's tent,
Centre-placed, is bright, besprent
    With the purple's royal dye ;

And at length a palace grows
Where the barbarous monarch shows
  Conquest in his blood-shot eye ;
Bridges o'er its streams are thrown
Rudely as it floweth down ;
O'er them pass wild nations on
  From a bleak and barren strand,
Like fierce stream to still lake, gone
  To a sunnier, sweeter land ;
While, alas ! the flooding tide
Is with gory crimson dyed,
As if Nature shed in pain
Bloody tear-drops, and not rain.

On yet flows the Stream of Time—
  Bluer depths and currents lighter,
Charmed by sweet romance of rhyme,
  Softer gleam and glow the brighter.
On it glows by tourney-plain
  Where the feudal barons meet,
Friendly force in arms to strain
And to lay the prize they gain
  At the fairest lady's feet.
Bright their arms ! as wave on wave
  Flows the tide of chivalry—

Banners floating o'er the brave ;
  Sounds of martial minstrelsy !
While, like foam-wreaths of cascade
  Flow their snow-white plumes, above
Seas of lances ; and the glade
  Is sweet with songs of war and love.

Thus, from the Provençal clime
  Of chivalry, love, arms, and song,
Onward flows the Stream of Time
  With a broader current strong ;
By the mill and by the cot ;
By baron's plain and yeoman's lot ;
And through the town where anvils ring,
And looms their wheels intricate fling ;
And where the burgher keepeth guard
In jerkin stout, as watch and ward,
And dons the steel-cap on his head,
  Whene'er the chartered rights he won
By skill, as by the blood he shed,
  Are threatened by the baron's son :
For, sheltered in his moated walls
  He spreads the flag of liberty,
With heart no tyranny appals,
  With stalwart arm and bosom free ;

While mill-fall waters cheerly chime,
As onward flows the Stream of Time.

On it flows and pauses never—
    Glory to its gushing tide !
Now an ocean—once a river ;
    How its billows leap in pride !
As through towns the streamlets glide,
Onwards shining to the seas,—
    So it flows, and on its bosom
    Bears the bud that has to blossom
All amid wild forest trees.
    On its breast, swelled to the gale,
    Commerce spreads her snow-white sail ;
On its ocean, ships of iron,
    Fed by fire, and breathing steam,
Every anchoring port environ—
    Before, by night, a fiery gleam—
Behind, by day, a sun-tinged cloud—
    Misty as the flag of dream !
Hopeful as the rainbow proud !
    Civilizing, bringing nearer,
    Joining lands and making dearer,
Linking poles and marrying nations,
    Bearing written messengers,

Fraught with love and aspirations :
    Doves with notes unto the stars !
Wires, which lead the electric fires
    From the distant heart to heart !—
Like sunrise on village spires,
    Beacons of the Better Part!
Racing time and conquering space,
    Flying on the wings of heaven,
Hallowing with life each place,
    Saving hours for goodness given,
Bidding war's red course to cease,
Harnessing the steeds of peace,
Driving them through sea and land
With a progress good and grand ;
Making way for that blest day
    When God's own sun indeed shall shine ;
And men all brethren, in its ray
    Shall share communion divine ;
For this the stream amid the rushes,
Purling, bubbling, tinkling gushes ;
For this the river from its fountain
Floodeth, foameth down the mountain ;
For this it streameth in commotion,
That it may flow into the ocean ;
For this—the course and end sublime
For which we float the Stream of Time.

ALBION.

As breathing storm and swelling surges wild,
Old Neptune swam the Deucalionian sea,
Before an island ranked its white-ribbed rocks
Above the surf of that tempestuous main;
Summer winds blew, and through his branchy veins
The fond warmth rose, as on his ocean path,
A wandering sea nymph, floating on her back,
Showed her white breasts like cliffs above the waves.
Swift he pursued: his deity all bright
With amorous fire, as when the burning sun
Kisses the shell-lips of the eastern main;
And soon his fingers tangled in the maze
Of the green tresses of her sea-weed hair,
And held her fast while the god pressed her sides,
And forth there sprung a giant youth who spread
His sinewy arms and dived into the deep;
Then rose—the foam-froth blowing from his mouth,

Shaking his locks and shouting to the storm,
While sea-mews wheeling wildly overhead
Waved their white wings, and shrieked forth "Albion."

                    The giant child
Played with the monsters of that stormy sea;
Hunted the porpoises till scarce they dared
Show their swine snouts and backs above the wave;
Spread forth his hands and grasped a herring shoal
And threw their quivering millions to the sky
To fall again in shower of silver scales,
Like wondrous rain into their mother sea;
And when the winds were wildest, then he best
Loved the stern wrestling with the water-snakes;
Held forth their coils when curled to close him round,
Then dived beneath and rose again, and forced
Their horny tails within their jagged jaws,
Till faint in one long line upon the top
Of the waves they floated—stretched a weary mile.
Or, when the child was tired with his play,
Then tore he from the ocean caves their growth,
And binding it in ropy meshes strong,
Caught the old whale and bridled him with them
And rode him, spouting floods and weltering wild,
Through the Atlantic to Pacific shores.

Yet most he chose
The Northern Ocean with cold breezes strong,
And heard the trumpet of its tempests swell
With glee, as heroes hear the shout of Mars.
Battle of billows, wild war of the waves,
Were his delight; and as he grew, his heart
Aspired to make him master of the sea—
Monarch of ocean ! for his ancient sire,
Great Neptune, died soon after he was born,
When the old faith perished from a widening world,
And left him heir of all his ocean halls,
His sea-weed bowers and monsters of the deep.

And thus he grew
In stature huge, as rock above the tide,
And strove to rule the ocean, and control
The sweeping gales that drove the galleys down ;
And quell the storms and stay the waterspouts
That rose in columns bright unto the sky,
Then broke in deluge wide and sunk again ;
Or quench the volcanic fires that through the wave
Flamed forth from fierce vent of the underground
Amid the waters raging unsubdued.

Ambition high
As this, throughout his sphere of mortal life,

Honoured the trident of his ocean power,
And mariners delighted in his sway.
But centuries passed, and he was growing old—
His green hair blanched, his body's channels dried;
When ere he died he lifted up a psalm
To the only One who always heareth prayer.
" Heaven," he cried, " who ever looketh down
Upon my waves ! if death may only be
A change of being, as thousand things declare,
Grant me such change from thy bright blue above
That I may yet immortally watch over
The seas I love, and in some other form,
And haply nobler way, rule o'er the waves,
At once their monarch and their guardian."

                    He said and died :
Not died, but changed ; standing above the waves ;
Breast high he stood above them as he changed ;
His shoulders wide and blade-bones straight became
White chalky rocks which hurled the sea-spray back ;
His breasts were hills ; his beard made fertile fields,
Such as the bearded barley yet should grace ;
Blue lakes his eyes became ; his furrowed face
Gave channels for the rivers ; while his hair
With high dense forests shaded all the land ;

And a new island stood amid the sea—
Hence Albion named ; hence raised to rule the waves
With nobler sway than the storm-quelling one,
Destined to found, from furthest shore to shore,
Though should storms blow the white-cliffed isle stands
      firm,
The rule of commerce and the reign of peace ;
And under the dominion of the sky,
To ever keep the empire of the sea.

THE LOVE OF LOCRINE.

I.

THE slashing and the clashing of the swords and
shields were over;
The wounds of the slain warriors red as ruby heads of
clover;
And Humber's mangled body was floating down the
river,
Which ever since has borne his name and bears it on
for ever.
And the routing and the shouting of victory were
ended,
And the cries of " Long live Locrine!" were in the air
suspended;
But the blaze of battle still upon his face was beaming,
As after blood-red sunset the northern lights flash
streaming.

And before their king they set the spoils that were the
    rarest;
And unto their king they brought the captives that
    were fairest;
But in the crowd a maid shone forth, in grief her
    white hands twining,
Like evening's star with sweet pale face and long locks
    yellow shining.
O fair and rare as ever were, were the eyes of young
    Estrilde,
And her face shone with as pure a light as a virgin
    silver shield ;
And with the arrows of her eye, and the shield of her
    pure look,
She vanquishèd the victor, and the captor captive took.

II.

O FORGETFUL, unregretful, are the sons of the All-
Father,
Though to rouse their memories often shall Thor his
thunders gather ;
And so Locrine forgot his troth, and that amid Cornish
men
The King of Cornwall's daughter dwelt, whom they
called Guendolen :
To her, not loth, he pledged his troth, when the snow
flakes were falling ;
And now he woos another maid, while the young birds
are calling ;
To her he swore by the berries white of the Druids'
misel-bush ;
And now again he pledges love, by the buds of the
blooming rush.
O, faithless to the deathless ! O, false and erring
brother !
He who deceives one maiden will also fail another.
Estrilde he loves, yet does not wed. O vain and
graceless men !
Fearing the king her father, he weds Guendolen.

III.

TERRIBLE is the clank-clank ; is the clank-clank of the
chain,
Which the wearied prisoner drags behind him—every
step in pain ;
But far more terrible than that chain are the fetters
stern that bind,
The loveless heart to the loveless heart, and unwilling
mind to mind.
Before the marriage moon had waned upon its circling
way,
Locrine and his bride Guendolen had many a clouded
day ;
She saw she was not loved, and he pined for his captive maiden,
Whom Humber slain, had brought from far, with his
sea treasure laden.
And the fair Estrilde had loved him, since she in his
eye found grace ;
(There were then no maids of Mary, but the Druids'
heathen race ;)

And her blood was warm though her skin was fair,
    and flushed up when he came,
As reddens the white morning star at the sun-god's car
    of flame.
And seven short years their hidden love in secret
    bower they tasted,
In wild lone spot where, ere they loved, the wood-
    bine's sweets were wasted;
Where her cheeks grew red as berries; her fingers as
    suckles fair,
And fronds of the fern curled forth their leaves, like
    tresses of her hair.
And 'twas there Locrine at midnight hour, leaving
    Guendolen,
Oft sought Estrilde's fair breast of love, amid that
    hidden glen;
As a stream speeds flowing underground, to meet
    another oft
All amid the bloom of blackness and the darkness fair
    and soft.
And as those streams swell brightly, when beneath
    the sunshine mingled,
So when they met in love's sunlight, their pulses rose
    and tingled;

And they together strayed the woods, or on the moss
lay down,
While her eyes gleamed through the hazels, with their
ripe nuts' own rich brown.
And they together sat at eve, listening the beetle's
drone,
Warning the gnats from the setting sun, to sleep
beneath the moon ;
And a little one at their feet reclined, or when they
called her name
From chasing the white miller moth, the maid Sabrina
came.

IV.

O, STOLEN things are sweetest, and hidden meetings
    meetest !

They say who have not seen the point which makes
    each round completest;

But kings are men and jewels fade, and thus erred
    Lord Locrine,

Though the son of Trojan Brutus, "sprung of old
    Anchises' line."

O, had he never heard his father tell the tale of Troy,

And how that glorious city fell from lust of girl and
    boy;

And how the hosts of long-haired Greeks rushed to
    Scamander's plain;

How god-like great Achilles raged and Hector warred
    in vain?

Her breast his rest, Estrilde he loved, and thought
    not of the morrow,

Which quickly came and brought with it beginning of
    his sorrow;

From Cornwall's land the news spread forth that
    Cornwall's king was dead,
And sadly mourned Guendolen and drooped her
    queenly head.
"To thine own people haste thee—thou shalt be my
    queen no more ;
Hence to Cornwall's savage people, and to Cornwall's
    rugged shore ;
From board and bed, I send thee !"—so said with
    wrathful face,
Locrine unto Guendolen, who sought her own brave
    race.
Then he turned unto Estrilde—"Up ! and take thy
    place," he cried ;
"Thou hast long reigned as my love, now reign as my
    queen and bride !"
O, justice most unjustly done, and kind yet cruel love !
Never two black-winged ravens can make one white-
    plumed dove.

V.

LIKE storm winds from the mountains, and like
    leaves blown from the west,
So fiercely and so many, with revenge in every breast;
With its tempest in their troops swift bearing them
    along,
Against Locrine the Cornish men marched in their
    thousands strong.
And as the fair moon reddens when the winds rise in
    the sky,
And fierce fire flashes o'er the earth from her once
    placid eye,
So fiercely did Guendolen lead on her nation's war,
With the wild-eyed black steeds of revenge speeding
    her scythed car.
O, where is now the arm of might which bore old
    Humber down,
And bade him ever weep in death, who living could
    but frown?
O, where is now that arm, Locrine? 'Tis palsied by
    thy side;
And now an arrow nails it there, while flows thy life's
    last tide;

And as before the swarming gulls, whose plumage in
    the sun
Shines silver, as their veering wings upon their prey
    have won,
The finny shoals dive deeply, and then spread beneath
    the wave—
So fled the troops of Locrine, and each strove his life
    to save.
O palsied was thy arm, Locrine! and recreant were
    thy band,
Because not then in honour's cause was drawn thy
    gleaming brand ;
Nor is thy loss thy own alone, but 'neath the gusty
    sky,
Not only fall thy dragon scales, but plumes of linnets
    lie !

VI.

WHAT two sweet birds flee o'er the meads before the
 fierce hawk's wing?
What two fair forms unto the stream before their foe-
 men spring?
What matron and what maiden into that wild stream
 are cast,
At the word of fierce Guendolen, rising above the
 blast?
The Severn gurgled weirdly, as into its oozy deep,
It drew those two fair forms—there evermore to sleep;
Sabrina, like a lily bud, just broken from the stem;
And Queen Estrilde a rose, when storm has frayed its
 diadem!
O, cruel was the deed! but its inspiration came
From one wronged and bleeding heart, and two jealous
 eyes of flame!
Love is cruel as the grave, and the trodden worm will
 sting,
And the stock-dove even has a plume—an arrow's
 flight to wing!

Yet, amid the waves of Severn one perished who was
    pure,
And thus her name in many a rhyme for ever shall
    endure ;
The stream, as murmuring on it flows, its syllables
    may lose,
But Maid Sabrina's name has life through Milton's
    tuneful throes.
And ne'er a bard by Severn's banks can wander gently
    on,
But now he hears a singing voice, and then again it's
    gone ;
Until at length his ear grows quick and all his soul is
    bound,
As Sabrina sings amid the stream in gushes of clear
    sound :
Of her parents' sin and death, and her own untimely
    fate,
She sings amid the ripples, as the water-flags relate ;
And the rushes bend and listen, and the birds as they
    fly by
Catch the ringing of her singing and the music of her
    sigh ;
The reeds upon the banks tell its notes unto the trees,
And swift the river flows along and gives them to the
    breeze.

And the poet hears the tale they tell, which all his
    spirit stirs;
And he weaves it into words of song, though not so
    sweet as hers.

DEEP UNTO DEEP.

DEEP unto deep loudly calleth, and solemnly rise their
tones,
With deafening roar and wildering wail, and miserable
moans ;
Like a sound from the nether bowels of earth's granitic
bones
When the fiery utterance reacheth to the highest
mountain cones ;
Like words of the stern old ocean full fathoms over
her stones,
Or, like wail of the inmost soul and its agonizing
groans.

Far out of her fiery vents, raves the voice of the earth,
    Ho! Ho!
The flames are in and around me and pass through me
    to and fro ;
And their steaming breath is upon me, as round and
    round I go,
And fierce, like tongues of hounds so red, they are hot
    upon their foe,
And, like tangled hissing yellow snakes, they wind
    about ; and, lo !
I parch, I scorch, I burn and live in the fierce consum-
    ing woe !

Forth from her surging waterspouts and her wide
    abyssmal jaws,
The words of the wrinkled ocean rise as from huge
    behemoth maws ;
In vain thou callest me, O earth ! to break the eternal
    laws,
And of thy dire deep wombed agony to quench the
    fiery cause ;
My tide flows forth, but it ebbs again to point frail
    human saws,
While that I reach I fail to keep, and I may not ever
    pause !

A cry comes from the innermost soul—Oh, woe! Oh,
    woe is me!

The fires of sin I fiercer feel than thy flames, O earth!
    to thee;

The wild volcanic passions surge with their waves of
    agony,

And the conscience seared with life's fell steam, but
    lava soon may be;

Its embers scorch with blackening blast full many a
    pleasant lea;

While all thy billows can never quench those fires of
    earth, O sea!

THE SORREL MEAD.

BLOOMING is yon meadow,
  This warm summer-tide,
Not a single shadow,
  Its rosy face to hide.

Buttercups nor daisies,
  Pearl nor gild the mead,
Elsewhere, in wild mazes,
  The flowery dance they lead.

Ruddy spikes of sorrel
  Overtop the grass,
Like red wreaths of coral,
  Or cheeks of lovely lass.

Seems, indeed, that Nature
  Chose this mead, her cheek ;
Chose it for the feature
  Best her charms to speak.

And that, modest-bred,
  When the sky looked on her ;
There blushed those blossoms red,
  In ruby light upon her.

SPRING AND NO SPRING.

SHE promised me all should be well,
  When came the next sweet spring;
The hyacinths blue should ring joy's bell,
  Love's dove should prune its wing.

The violets—those blue eyes of May,
  Vie with the turtle's wing,
And sue her dark eye's dazzling ray:
  But not for me—there's spring.

I must distrust my sense, not her;
  I have dreamed it is spring-tide;
Winter, in its white minever,
  Yet reigns in chilling pride.

Shines no May sun: bloom no May flowers,
  The birds no love-notes sing;
Been no March winds, no April showers:
  Oh, not for me there's spring!

.

THE SACRIFICE OF THE KING.

MIGHTY woe was over Norland,
  Famine laid her sons earth under,
Stalked o'er forest, hill, and moorland;
  Sighed the wind and moaned the thunder.

Mightier woe came Norland over,
  Drought her sods to dry dust crumbling,
Parching tree, herb, grass, and clover;
  Whistled wind, the thunder rumbling.

Mightiest woe for Norland followed,
  Dropped her blade the foe's foot under;
In the mire her cravens wallowed;
  Shrieked the wind and groaned the thunder.

Then arose the Scald, age-hoary,
  Pointing to the heavens louring:
" See," he cried, " the Gods of glory
  Frown in wrath on Norsemen cowering!

"See," he cried, "the horse of Woden
    Frets, and ramps the clouds asunder!
Hark, the angry skies are loaden
    With the Hammer-Bearer's thunder!

"Mighty Thor is wroth, and Frega,
    'Mid her naked-bosomed daughters,
Rends her gold locks, while her eager
    Eyes pour forth the whelming waters.

"Famine, Drought, Defeat, Dishonour,
    Wake the thunders of high heaven:
Land, whose sins lie heavy on her,
    Weak the toil your life to leaven!

"Poor the blood and vain the slaughter,
    Warriors, ye have shed and taken:
Land, whose sins have curses brought her,
    Give your best or die forsaken.

"People, who in vain have striven,
    Richest thread of life now sunder,
Yield your King's blood unto Heaven!"
    Howled the wind and roared the thunder.

Spake the Scald.   The people shouted,
" Yea, the King we yield to Heaven :
We, the brave, yet we, the routed :"
Piled are stones, and oaths are given.

Keen the knife ; the Blood free floweth,
Freshening earth above and under ;
Smile the Gods ; the sunshine gloweth ;
Stilled the winds and ceased the thunder !

THE SNOW MAIDEN.

Dark was the winter night,
  And the storm blew gustily,
When, amid its restless watches,
  A maiden came to me.

Her shoulders bare, gleamed white,
  And were bright, but cold to see;
The curve of her shape was wavy
  As snow-wreaths curling free.

Icicles were her eyes,
  And her body glittered fair;
What, but wreaths on the frosted pane,
  Could gleam as gleamed her hair?

Morning came, and yellow
  The light of the young sun shone;
As fell the flakes from the hedges,
  My maiden white was gone.

O, my poor snow maiden,
  Swift gone in the warm sunshine!
So may each cold thought go with thee,
  That chilleth me or mine.

THE NECKLACE, BRISING.

On the bosom fair, what resteth there,
　On the bosom softly rising?
Upon Freyja's breast, what there doth rest,
　But the golden necklace, Brising?

From the hearth-stone has her Odur gone,
　And for him she is ever pining;
And every tear turned a golden sphere,
　Is amid her necklace shining.

She travels west, and she takes no rest,
　But towards the south is speeding;
She travels east, and will make no feast,
　Till northward her husband leading.

And with every stop her tears down drop,
   And change into beads all golden;
Until larger grows and brighter glows
   The string on her bosom folden.

And never a dame had jewelled flame
   With a light more brightly glowing,
Than Freyja bore, when 'twas thus she wore
   The tears with her heart's-gold flowing.

No jewels rare can ever compare
   With gems from the heart's fount rising;
And 'tis Fate's award, who mourns her lord
   Shall wear Freyja's necklace, Brising.

THE CHERRY-COLOURED RIBBONS.

THE fairest maiden, to my sight,
  She wears a charming bonnet,
And cherry-coloured ribbons bright
  Are choicely twined upon it:
Those cherry-coloured ribbons
  Shine brighter, to my eyes,
Than blushes and flushes
  That deck the morning skies.

They bring a morning to my heart,
  And when I see them glow
In lane, or field, or street, or mart,
  My sun is risen, I know:
Those cherry-coloured ribbons
  Are but the rosy dawn
Whence gleameth and beameth
  Her sunny face of morn.

And, as all nature riseth up
　The rosy dawn to greet,
And every flower lifts high its cup
　Morn's glowing beams to meet,—
Those cherry-coloured ribbons
　My pulses fondly move,
And heating and beating,
　My heart swells up with love.

Yet not to them she owes the grace
　Which sets my pulse on fire ;
When flush the blushes of her face
　Their hues fade and expire :
Those cherry-coloured ribbons
　Are but her ministers,—
The graces have faces,
　But not so bright as her's !

Were ever eyes so brightly dark,
　Was ever smile so sweet ?
O that my ear might always mark
　The music of her feet !
Those cherry-coloured ribbons
　But her bright morn declare ;
Aurora, adore her,
　Thy face is not so fair !

And O, the soul within those eyes,
  Amid that smile—the heart ;
Fade, ruddy morning, from the skies,
  Ere they from me depart :
Those cherry-coloured ribbons
  Forth angel-banners fling,
And given is Heaven
  To those who pray and sing !

THE WOES OF LOVE.

'TIS not all bliss to love as truly,
  Dear one, as I love thee;
Howe'er the sky may beam forth bluely,
  There's brine amid the sea.

The dark delay—the anxious trial;
  The watching for a glance;
The craving fierce—the faint espial,
  Which wills yet fears advance.

The staff of hope which strongly bore us
  A moment gladly on;
Instantly snapped, falling before us—
  Failing, broken, and gone.

The sleepless night—the timid dawning
  Which yet but gleameth gray;
The bitter prayer which begs a morning
  For Love's far brighter day.

The fond wish with no plumes to wing it,
    The pensive, sad suspense,
Like bell flower waiting breeze to ring it,
    Yet silent to the sense.

The feeding on the heart—the fretting;
    The waiting for a word,
Which comes perhaps like sunlight setting,
    Or, like a severing sword.

Hid in the heart—the jaundice jealous;
    The pride of poverty;
Consuming demons, all too zealous
    Their master's slaves to be.

Scorching the soul—the fire of passion
    With a red glow intense,
Yet such as angel's eye might flash on
    To light the clouds of sense.

All this, and more, there could be newly
    Rent from the heart's red tree,
Shows 'tis not bliss to love as truly,
    Dear one, as I love thee.

THE BLINK OF BLUE.

THE dim mists hide
The mountain's side,
The sunshine glints but faintly through
The darkling clouds
Which gloom in crowds ;—
O for a bonny blink of blue !

Soft gleams of green
On slopes are seen
Which slant upon our highland view ;
But showers pour down
On heather brown ;—
O for a bonny blink of blue !

Thy eyes, July !
In dim mists lie—
Those eyes of warmest azure hue !
O dry those showers,
Ye heavenly powers !—
O for a bonny blink of blue !

And you, ye clouds,
Which come in crowds,
Above the nations who yet rue
The floods of ill,
And storms which kill ;—
O for a bonny blink of blue !

The earth is mist ;
The clouds make tryst
Around it, and obscure our view ;
O for the gleam
Of heaven's beam :
O for its bonny blink of blue !

7161

THE MUSIC THAT SHALL BE.

FROM heaven comes the sound,
　O'er earth it rings with glee,
Above, beneath, around,—
　The music that shall be!
The south shall kiss the north,
　The west shall kiss the east;
The hills to the vales go forth,
　The greatest be the least;
The channel be dried low,
　And France and England one;
And in one stream shall flow
　The Danube and the Don;
Shall cease each earthly jar,
　The crow like thrush sing free;
And never discord mar
　The music that shall be.

M

The strains are tuning low,
. But soon those strains shall rise,
And earth's ear overflow
With music of the skies;
And man with man shall stand
Beneath the glowing sun,
Together hand in hand,
The many joined in one;
And rivers flow with milk,
And rocks the honey pour,
And trees be robed with silk,
And deserts flush with flower:
Shall cease each mortal jar—
Each song an angel-glee;
Nor any discord mar
The music that shall be!

BLACK GANG CHINE.

———

PATH of darkness! road of night!
   Black Gang Chine!
Way of gloom for cataract bright
   Unto the brine!
Thine the dizzy height, the edge
   Of wondrous line,
Whirling on its Mammoth ledge,
   Black Gang Chine!
Thine the black rock; thine the chasm;
   Thine the vast spine,
High, wide, and growthless; born of spasm!
   Monster divine!
Thine dark beauty, wooing tender,
   Like Moorish lips!
Thine dark grandeur; thine the splendour
   Of an eclipse!
Thine the path of grand dark spirit,
   Lost to the divine,
Fallen from that it did inherit—
   Black Gang Chine!

THE GERMAN PROVERB.

"To-day red—to-morrow dead :"
So the German proverb said.
Gretchen heard it to her sorrow,
Going to the ball to-morrow ;—
Looking in the glass, to see
Red and white so well agree.

"To-day red—to-morrow dead :"
So the German proverb said.
Wilhelm laughed and said, We may :
Better, then, have joy to-day ;
Crack the walnuts, pass the wine,—
Die, perhaps, but living, dine.

"To-day red—to-morrow dead :"
So the German proverb said.
While the Frau, of age fourscore,
Only told her beads the more ;
Saying age was made of sorrow,
And she prayed a good to-morrow.

"To-day red—to-morrow dead :"
So the German proverb said.
While the party all around
Gave the words a separate sound,
As life's eve was growing cold,
Or its dawn was eastern gold.

"To-day red—to-morrow dead :"
So the German proverb said.
And the preacher added, Then,
Live so as to live again ;
Live well here, nor make your sorrow ;
Live to-day and live to-morrow.

OLD MAN AND YOUNG.

UNKNIT thy furrowed brows, old man!
  And loose thy puckered lips;
The golden sun gilds evening dun;
  Old earth the new dew sips;
And why should'st thou die dark, old man,
  In pride of pomp or pelf,
And scorn the beam which young eyes dream,
  Nor see the snake in self?

Say not in treacherous tones, old man!
  That wisdom is in years;
When on the ground the seed is found
  Shed from the burnished ears;
And of those ears thus shed, old man!
  The empty husks remain;
While even the seed to spring at need
  Is old life young again.

It is not childish talk, old man !
   Those dizzy dreams of youth,
Whose rainbows ray, whose pinions play
   Upon the breath of truth.
There's fount of colour deep, old man !
   From whence those rainbows rise,
And curving springs, whence plumy wings
   Soar singing to the skies.

Prate not so much of age, old man !
   'Tis modest not, nor true ;
There's even dust despised, which must
   Be older far than you ;
And think a moment, pray, old man !
   That power is old as HIM
Whose endless truth has ever youth,
   Whose love grows never dim !

And hast thou ever read, old man !
   How youth came from the skies,
And filled the morn on which 'twas born
   With oldest harmonies ?
And taught that such as thou, old man !
   Must yet be born again ;
And scorning wise, all ancient lies,
   Held children up to men.

Shake not thy palsied head, old man !
   It readeth thus to me :
Immortal Truth, Eternal Youth,
   Live one in harmony.
Truth never dies, mark well, old man !
   We die to Truth and Love ;
And suns that set, shall burnish yet
   The blushing skies above.

Say not what is—will be, old man !
   That change is not ordained,
That slaves and kings are useful things,
   And men are happiest chained.
The breezes freely flow, old man !
   By no vain edict bound ;
The starry choir pronounce thee liar !
   And roll more radiant round.

Then totter to thy tomb, old man !
   Nor strive again to freeze
The warming flood of rich red blood,
   Which fills our ministries ;
Thy place is underground, old man !
   Thy tomb shall have a tongue ;
The young grass grow o'er thee below—
   The skies beam o'er the young.

Old things must go with thee, old man !
 Old dynasties must die ;
Old creeds, old laws, " the good old cause,"
 Make sunset in the sky ;
New thoughts are rising high, old man !
 And still the prophets sing—
The birth of truth—the faith of youth,
 And sunshine of the Spring.

I.

———•———

I ! I !   Who am I ?
A speck on the dusty road-side dry ;
A passing breath on the viewless air ;
Here and There in the Everywhere ;
A little sound and a little stir,
And the print of the foot of a sojourner :
        I, I ; that am I—
Child of the clay who am passing by !

I ! I !   Who am I ?
A spark from the star-wheels of the sky ;
A breath which the winds bear far and wide ;
A voice whose echoes ever abide ;
Not dust below, but a light afar,
With the flash of the trail of a traveller :
        I, I ; that am I—
Heir of the joys of the upper sky !

EYES OF BROWN.

Eyes of blue may sweetly pierce,
Eyes of black are quick and fierce ;
But the eyes whose power I own,
Are my lady's eyes of brown.

When in motion, liquid light,—
Softly dark and darkly bright,—
Like a stream o'er red-mossed stone,
Gleams in amber 'mid their brown.

When at rest, their shades are deep,
As if meaning great they keep ;
As a tarn on mountain high
Seems that it would hold the sky.

Dark as any tarn are they,
When lit from the gates of day,
Clearer brims its cup, and fills
Up the grand hush of the hills.

Like twin mountain tarns, her eyes,
Solitary sanctities,
Musing 'mid ways seldom trod,
Up amid the hills of God.

Yet so large,—so soft their orbs,
All the heaven she absorbs,
From their fringes shines again
In the path God walks with men.

Oh, to look up to those eyes
Well might make the sceptic wise !
And might teach him how the light
Gleameth through the darkest night.

Simpler cares to them belong :
Not less worthy, though, of song :
Glance of kindness in distress,
Look of love, to soothe and bless.

All the care to watch and ward,
All the womanly regard,—
All the upturned gaze of prayer,
In those eyes of brown are there.

Let the blue eyes sweetly pierce,
Let the black ones sparkle fierce ;
But the eyes whose power I own,
Are my lady's eyes of brown !

THE LITTLE BOAT.

A LITTLE boat lay in a little cove,
And the stream flowed level by,
And above the silver-grey rocks arose,
And above the wide, dim sky.

And upon the grey rock the thick trees spread,
And hung o'er the hill's grim breast,
Tangled and matted, and massy and wild,
As the hair on a giant's chest.

But the little cove was a still, sweet place,
Like dimple in toil-worn cheek,
And the little boat lay as gently there
As a smile in dimple meek.

And around that cove the lady-fern grew
And unfurled the brown-curled frond
Into tressy leaves, whose long ringlets fair
Suggested a face beyond.

While the coarser bracken and broad hart's-tongue
Hung their locks to right and left,
And the rock-spleenwort and the bright club-moss
Spread rife in that ferny cleft.

And the little boat lay in that small cove,
Ready, though waiting and still,
Like a thought conceived in a poet's brain,
Or a fond wish in the will.

O, let the brave thought swim forth in a song,
And float on the stream of sound ;
And O, let the fond wish be borne to her
For whom its course is bound.

And the little boat from the little cove
O'er the waters gaily range,
For everything speaks of everything,
And nothing to aught is strange.

NEVER FEAR.

THOUGH the clouds are black as night,
Never fear ;
Though the lightning's dazzling bright,
Never fear ;
Though the thunderbolt is red,
Though the shaft of death is sped,
God is present overhead ;—
Never fear !

Though the tyrant's axe is bright,
Never fear ;
Though the black block is in sight,
Never fear :
Though a foeman is each knave,
Though a coward is each slave,
God is with the freeman brave ;—
Never fear !

Though the bigots curses raise,
    Never fear ;
Though the martyrs' fagot blaze,
    Never fear :
Though their souls are void of ruth,
Though they strive to cripple youth,
God is ever with the Truth ;—
    Never fear !

Though the Storm-God flaps his wings,
   . Never fear ;
Though the tempest death-song sings,
    Never fear :
In the clouds are blue specks fair,
Through the dark bough blows the air,
God is present everywhere ;—
    Never fear !

NEW YEAR VERSES.

O DEATH, thou door of life,—thou shadowy porch
Of new existence!—once again thy portals
Open, and once again thy flickering torch
    Guideth to the immortals.
The insect hours beneath thy chilly breath,
Droop their grey wings, and close their tiny plumes ;
The days are hearsed up in thy nightsome glooms :
The ghosts of years troop unto thee, O Death !
Sad waves the mournful, melancholy willow
Over the stream of Time's last sunken billow ;
But ripple follows ripple, wave on wave,
And morn's young eyes from out the orient glow
When night's cowl darkest glooms upon its brow,
While spectral shades sink into the deep grave,
Shimmering and melting like thin flakes of snow
On the dark waters, where the eddies rave,
Though all the buds of earth rise up to blow.

Dim porch of Time! amid God's shadowy wood,
Pillared with moonstone, indistinct and thin,
And branched around with a cloud-woven screen,
Slim as a mist-bower, morning's sky within :
Impalpable as void, thou long hast stood,
While thro' thee bards have rather felt than seen,
As over thee a web-winged Instant hung,
Bat-like and weird, thy filmy mists among :
A fading shade,—a spectre like a wind,
Failing in ebbing gusts,—and like a lung
Drawn inward by a respiration blind,
As though a fainting, breezy look was flung
By that vague Ghost of the Old Year behind ;
While by it passed, as two thoughts in a mind
Flit by each other, a Bright Spirit fair,
Like a fresh breath of odorous sun-filled air
With hastening eyes, and front-blown tresses bright ;
And, with a gush of music, rising higher,
And softly floating nigher, and yet nigher,
The soul of the New Year arose in light.

Thro' its fond eyes, so sweet in its bright hair,
I see the larch's tassels waving fair,
The old oak's sprouts of green, the pine's red birth,
The sycamore's rich gummy growth so pale ;—

Its pulse has quickened all things of the earth ;
Made dew from snow, and soft rain from the hail.
Thro' its fond eyes I see the bell of the vale ;
A bud, and then a bloom within that dell,
Where in the nutty copse I hear the tale
The blackbird yet shall pipe, with mellow swell.
The pink buds of the briar I smell them blow ;
I see the spotted cowslips gild the croft,
I hear the lark singing from heaven aloft ;
The very bee-flower blooms, and, bending low,
I strive to catch the insect form, and lo !
Within my hand the lovely petals glow !
I see the dark moss greened upon the eaves ;
I find the violet hid amid its leaves ;
I scent the grasses in the new-mown hay ;
    I bind the golden sheaves ;
    My fancy rushes weaves
Even as I sit and think on New Year's day !

I sit alone ; far, far from thee, O World,
Thou tyrant and thou slave ! Thou base deceiver
From nature and her ways, whose lip is curled
Even at thy mother's bosom. Thou bereaver,
Both false and foul, of all pure sweets of life,
I sit alone, even at thy midst, in strife

With thee and thine. I would I were a bird,
To fly away, far in some copse of nut,
And there, amid the dim still evening, shut,
When naught but God and some fond traveller heard,
　　To pipe a mournful ditty,
　　Such as might move to pity
Of thee and thine, all whom thy woe had stirred !

Such song may sound, if not by me be sung,
God never yet hath lacked the thrushes' tongue ;
Yet while I sit alone on this New Year,
Like Crusoe, notching at my tree of woe,
My thoughts, like his, in this my isle so drear,
Must back into my own lone bosom flow,
Reflect on time misspent, on time forgot,
On moments lost, and hours I yet must gain,
And while I bless the white days of the lot,
Reckon the long hours I have spent in vain :
How many sad hours I have lost in sleep ;
How many dark hours have been sunk in sin ;
How oft forgot my father's flock to keep,
How oft allowed the wolf to enter in :
So many acres have I left untilled
Of that fair glebe my father to me gave ;
So many waggons have remained unfilled,

Though ripe brown corn in many a field doth wave;
So many vain words have I falsely spoken;
So many vows of goodness have been broken;
So many prayers unsaid and hymns unsung;
So many restless Sabbaths of my folly;
So many falterings of the priestly tongue;
So many thorns in my unberried holly;
So many thoughts to man and earth's poor sod;
    So few to heaven and God!
Bad as the world is,—black as is its shame,
    Yet am not I to blame?
Judge not, O Man, but to thyself be true,
And the world's judgment shall be read in you!

Hail, Hope! I love thy neighbourly abode,
And aye will journey thy frequented road,
For all glad thoughts are warbled from thy tongue,
    Thou New Year's Ode!
Thou art for ever, ever, ever sung,
Even by the way-worn and the grey-beard young;
If I, inspired by thee, this New Year's day
Have seen young white lambs in the pastures play,
    Have seen the springtide flowers:
The bramble-bloom, the daisy's golden eye;
The silvery lady-smock, and crowfoot gay;

The purple cuckoo-buds, and hare-bells shy ;
The bright red pimpernel, and snowy may ;
    Have seen the springtide bowers :
The ripening briar-hip, and the ash's keys ;
The proud oak's acorns, and the fir's brown cones ;
The willow leaves blithe dancing in the breeze ;
And heard the woodlands sweet, with chirping tones
From song-birds' throats, in a rich concert given,
    As poet-praise to heaven !
If I, inspired by thee, have seen these bowers ;
    Have scented these fair flowers ;
Have heard these birds their mellow music raise,
    Through windows frosted o'er,
    Though snow has blocked the door,
Say, shall I sever Man from Nature's genial ways ?
O, no : O, never ! Hard as is man's dust
Of earthly being, he, too, has a spring,
Which, like the slender snow-drop, thro' the crust
    Of frozen earth and chill,
Shall gently rise a pure, transparent thing,
    And its spring-life fulfil !

Then grace to thee, New Year, and many a blessing,
    Old friend with a new face !
Glorious may be the days of thy possessing
    If we the moments grace.

The hours gone by we never can restore,
Their golden sands are scattered on the floor :
The days now lost we but lament in vain,
Their ruddy suns will never flush again :
The past is dead ; the present only lives ;
    The future but may be !
Never or Now ! To-day alone God gives,—
    To-day requires of thee.
To-morrow never comes ! This day shall be,
With a new life, the best New Year to thee !

HER DAY.

Sweetly now she sleepeth; Dreams, be bright and fair!
Snowy breast, swell lightly; Breath, enrich the air!
Morning, gently wake her; Winds, your softest sigh!
Dews and vapours, vanish; Sunshine, fill the sky!

Beaming now in beauty; Flowers, rise round her feet!
Grass, spring up all grateful; Bless her footsteps fleet!
Golden noon, look on her; Clouds, her presence flee!
Bluest heaven in her eye; Sun, your rival see!

Meekly now she resteth; Day, be still and pray!
Softening shadows, gather; Flickering fancies, play!
Western skies, in purple Glowing glory fade!
Evening star, beam o'er her, Twilight thro' thy shade!

Fondly now she sleepeth; Love, be watch and ward!
Lilies are her eyelids; Rose, whom no thorns guard!
Holy night, thus keep her; Sleep, refresh her charms!
God, still sweeter make her, folded in my arms!

THE REPUBLIC OF LETTERS.

———•———

REPUBLIC of Letters! Breaker of Fetters!
 Thine be the glory beneath the moon :
All things of splendour their homage render ;
 Thou rulest the world without a throne.
The bird that twitters, the beam that glitters,
 Sweet song and brightness unto thee give ;
Each vale and highland, each rock and island,
 Bring thee the first-fruits of all that live.

O hail her, Nature ! each living creature,
 Each blossom that fades, but not to fall
Without expressing a balmy blessing,
 Sweet in its scent, on its funeral pall !
Each singing fountain, each mighty mountain,
 For ye are parts of her wide domain ;
All things of motion ; thou, glorious Ocean ;
 And you, ye worlds of the heavenly plain !

Ye people, praise her, for Czar and Kaiser,
    All lawless else, must attend her will ;
And the fell lictors of earth's stern victors
    Shake at a stroke of her grey-goose quill :
Your blood-stained heroes and cruel Neroes,
    Girt with their cohorts of sword-armed men,
May never stagger beneath the dagger,
    But yet be pierced by her good steel pen !

Sing out with gladness, O world of sadness,
    For in her sweet land of light are free
All those who muster in glorious cluster
    To read the names on her noble tree :
Both man and woman, and lord and yeoman,
    In equal radiance thus may shine,
Write forth their story in words of glory,
    And ever live in each lustrous line !

Arise, O Honour ! and rest upon her,
    And cheer her sons, and her daughters bless ;
Around thee rallied, their brows are pallid,
    But a laurel leaf is within each tress ;
Though poor and sighing, and weak and dying,
    Some of them yet in the body stay ;
Within them folden is treasure golden,
    And strength to live in the years away.

Shout out, ye people, from hill and steeple,
   And own her sway and her ranks extend ;
Cry, Heaven speed her !   Of millions leader ;
   The tyrants' foe and fair freedom's friend !
Chains that are galling soon shall be falling
   When she rules over the minds of men ;
Her types shall rattle, her presses battle,
   And sword and sceptre shall be the pen !

Fade, night and darkness, and cold and starkness,
   With blear-eyed ignorance, flee away !
Knowledge glorious, rise victorious ;
   Waken, ye lands, with the dawning day.
The foe of fetters, the Rule of Letters,
   See, over all how its reign extends ;—
Upward and onward, skyward and sunward ;
   Bless we the Great Republic's friends !

MINE, AND OURS.

Mine, is the little hand, puny and weak ;
Ours, are the thousand arms, mountains to break :
Mine, is the atom of clay for the grave :
Ours, is the earth, with hill, valley, and wave :
Mine, will soon vanish, like corpse in the sod ;
Ours, will arise to the heaven of God !

Mine, is the secret prayer, breathed low and lone ;
Ours, is the anthem of conquering tone :
Mine, is the little flower, nurtured in dearth ;
Ours, are the blossoming Edens of earth :
Mine, will soon vanish, like corpse in the sod ;
Ours, will arise to the heaven of God !

Mine, is the brain, that but gleams like a spark ;
Ours, are the thoughts, like stars lighting the dark :

Mine, is the heart that beats, fearfully hurled!
Ours, are the heart-throbs that gladden the world :
Mine, will soon vanish, like corpse in the sod ;
Ours, will arise to the heaven of God!

Mine, is the hermit-life, lone in its hours ;
Ours, are humanity's loves, thoughts, and powers :
Mine, scarcely mine, is this frame, doomed to fall ;
Ours, is our God, common Parent of all :
Mine, will soon vanish, like corpse in the sod ;
Ours, will arise to the heaven of God!

SALVADORA.

THE morn was white-browed, softly fair,
With dewy pearls amid her hair,
And, purely sweet, the air was calm,
While hymned the lark its matin psalm,
When, as the first faint eastern blush,
                              Salvadora !
Lit up with rainbowed dews each bush,
I first beheld thy pale face flush,
                              Salvadora !

We met upon the dewy lawn,
We met beside the bloomy thorn ;
Her foot seemed loth to brush the dew,
And, pitying, passed the pasture through ;
And if by chance she shook the bough,—
                              Salvadora !
And with morn's tears fell blossoming snow,
She shrunk as though she caused them woe ;—
                              Salvadora !

We loved; we loved! as much as she
Could spare from all she gave to me;
Not that her love was given to change,
Or that her sated heart would range;
But that love was the soul in thee,

                Salvadora!

And from the bird upon the tree,
Rose up to God eternally,—

                Salvadora!

She loved bird, beast, and tiniest thing,
She loved leaf, bud, and blossoming;
She loved pure mirth and holy grief,
The green branch and the yellow leaf,
The quivering wing and proud pine's nod,—

                Salvadora!

The mountain ridge and valley sod,
But most was turned thy soul to God,

                Salvadora!

And when her pale face flushed with wrath
At wicked deeds, which darkened forth,
The seraphs never blushed above,—
Her anger pure was sacred love;
Thy soul it yet was white within,

                Salvadora!

Thy use on earth did then begin,—
Thou lovedst the sinner, not the sin,
Salvadora !

She loved the man, but not the king ;
She loved the soul, but not the thing ;
She loved the true apostles' feast,
But not the hand of useless priest :
Thy feet in daily duty trod,
Salvadora !
Thy reason had a monarch's nod,
Thy soul a temple was of God,
Salvadora !

Her cheek was pale as that white star
Which heralds first the eve from far,
And though its blush would faintly flood,
Its light was eloquent as blood ;—
Thy eye was wild and fitful bright,
Salvadora !
It seemed to wander thro' the night,
And yet it had the seraph's flight,—
Salvadora !

She passed away, like morning dews
Beneath the sun, in rainbow hues,

And, like those dews, she left behind
A fresher path, a purer wind;
For as the heaven-lost lark doth pour,
　　　　　　　Salvadora!
Unseen by us, her singing shower,
Thy memory had its music's dower,
　　　　　　　Salvadora!

I could not shriek, I could not rave;
I knew thou wert not in the grave:
Thy Soul was Thee, and that was Trust,
And Love and Truth, and never Dust;
Thy beauty was eternity,
　　　　　　　Salvadora!
Thy truth it was infinity,
Thy love was immortality,
　　　　　　　Salvadora!

Yet vast my loss! a broken vase,
Its perfume had diffused thro' space;
I scented odorously the air,
But never more the vase was there;
And yet I could not sigh nor groan,
　　　　　　　Salvadora!

Beneath the sun, beneath the moon,
I only was alone—alone,
                    Salvadora !

The sickening sense of solitude
Weighed like an atmospheric load ;—
Towns busy, cities thronged, were dull,
And peopled streets unbeautiful :
Faces were blank ;—thine not to me,
                    Salvadora !
In crowds I lacked society,
In multitudes I saw not thee,
                    Salvadora !

Thy Soul was Thee, and that was Trust,
And Love and Truth, and never Dust :
Beneath the sun, beneath the moon,
I only was alone—alone !
Alone—alone ! and yet unshriven,
                    Salvadora !
Alone—alone ! whilst thou wert given
The Spouse of God, the Bride of Heaven,
                    Salvadora !

A WINTER'S DRIVE IN DEVON.

THE morn is fine,—wind south, and blowing warm,—
The bright bays start upon the rutless road ;
Up hill and down hill whirl the merry wheels,
As Light-of-heart, thro' life's like changes runs;
While on each side, the orchards, pastures, fields,
O'er the high hedges lead the wandering glance,
To hills, vale-openings, and the waters blue.

Like senators of Nature's council-chamber,
The orchard trees, as if in conclave, stand,
Their venerable heads with blanched-moss covered,
And bearded with grey lichen down their trunks :
A reverend sight, a solemn, silvery scene
Of antique wisdom.   Wisely argue they
Of what new effort age can best produce,

Of energy that yet is in their pith,
Of duty of the aged to show the young
They yet are fertile in the fruits of life,—
Of brave old standards that had borne to the death,
Examples even to them they also told ;
And the soft sap like heated blood ran quick
From their hearts' cores to their branches, as they
    vowed   [names.
Young stocks and new grafts well should know their
And thus they dreamed, those reverend senators
In wint'ry robes, of spring again to come,
Of sprouts, sweet birds, green leaves, and reddening
    blooms ;
Of bowers of blossom, and of autumn's fruit
Filling deep vats with the apple's purest wine ;
And even of other brighter springs to come,
In whose warm suns the land would bloom more bright,
And all the young trees of the earth rejoice :
Though those fair springs would only green their graves,
Yet of them dreamed those patriarchal seers ;—
O, would our senators were wise as they !

Ho ! drag the wheels,—down hill the horses go :
There's rain in the wind,—it blows both hard and
    warm.

A swift shower falls ;—April in January !
The sun gleams forth, the valley opens wide !
We cross a bridge 'neath which a river braids
Its pearly twine with the moist, grassy banks,
From whence green pastures spread, while upward
    swells,
As far as eye can reach, the black, ploughed land,
Crowned with a grove of pines, like sentinels
Which watch o'er all, while here and there we catch
Glimpses of scenery which tempt the hands
To lines of landscape, notes for memory !

There, underneath, the river runneth blue ;
Upriseth from its brim the rough, red rock,
Bright from the rain, while slopeth by its side
The deep, black, ploughed land ; and, above the head
Of the ruddy rock, a slip of pasture green,
Bearing grey trees, adds brightness to the whole,
And brings a colouring of cheerfulness
To winter's face, which rarely glows more bright
Than where the ruddy rocks of Devon blush.

O earth, dear earth ! why are thy cloven sides
So deeply red ?   Perhaps we only mock thee,
Singing—thou blushest at thine own bright beauty ;

Singing—thy cheeks are rosy rife with health,
Or red with joyfulness ! If thou shouldst bleed,
Perchance thou bleedest ? Hast had cause to bleed ?
Perchance, O Land, when civil broil divided
Thy human children, thou wast wounded deep,
And yet unhealed remain ? Perchance of old,
In the wild British times or Saxon age,
Thus hast thou suffered ? or,—O terrible thought !—
When the dire Druids shed the innocent blood
To superstition's idols, thou receivedst it,
And givest it back again to tell the tale
Unto the vision pure of merciful heaven ;
And thus thou bleedest !

On, tramp, tramp ! we go ;
Shining at once there are two lamps i' the sky,—
More miles we have spent in musing than in seeing,—
The sun is westering, while the pallid moon,
So thin and ghost-like, rises timidly,
Like the lorn spectre of a deadened world,
To warn our worldlings of the fate of error !
Yet still light glows, and down the deep-cut roads
Trot our brave bays ; the setting sun red beaming
On window-panes of road-side cottages,
Green nesting nooks with myrtle on their walls,—
Retreats of rustic grace for musing minds,—

Economy's own palaces, where well
Great Independence, king of his own spirit,
His court may hold of hopes, and thoughts, and plans,
Wherewith to bless the empire of the soul;
While friendly at his loving levée wait
Truth, Faith, and Quiet,—nobles of his realm,—
With coroneted Hope and white-robed Peace!

Crack! goes the whip. Home, home! is now the wish,
The pyxies soon will at their revels be,
Sliding on moonbeams down upon the earth,
To foot it featly on the crisp sere leaves
Which floor the winter ball-room which they love;
Or floating down the freshets as they flow,
Bathing their loveliness, which whoe'er sees
His vision hurts if he should tell the tale:
For nature has her secrets, to be felt
In the quiet heart,—in the solitary soul,
And they who trill her briskest on the tongue
Have oft ne'er heard the whispers of her voice;
And few are they who list her bosom beat,
Or count the pulses of her passionate frame.

Home, home, we come! Flee far all nature's scenes!
Fade, day in Devon! Glories of all shires,

Your suns may set !   Where'er the place may be,
Home is the heart-spot, and the solemn rites
Around its hearthstone altar are more sweet
Than all the fumes of flowers and strains of song,
And pilgrim hymns which Nature's temple bless.

GENIUS.

AMONG the leaves spread of a strawberry bed
 Was a living and delicate tomb,
Which, under the rich fruit so fragrant and red,
 Hung in web of a frail insect loom ;
And a spirit was there in that sepulchre fair,
 And had panted within itself long,
Like the frail-shrouded soul of some genius rare,
 Or like bard who would live in sweet song.

The bright sun it shone the rich red fruit upon,
 And lit up with a beam that thin tomb,
And the stir of a life, faintly coming—then gone,—
 And now seeking for light in the gloom ;
And then, with a gentle pulse, rising in power,
 Throbbed forth in that sepulchre dim,
Like the soul of a Genius waiting its hour
 When the sunshine was beaming for him.

The sun it rose high, and its warmth floated nigh
   The frail tomb in the strawberry leaves,
And the tomb was a cradle for infancy's sigh,
   And a cot with a thaw in the eaves ;
And an emerald eye and a rich feathered thigh,
   And a soft, dim-hued winglet appeared,
Like young bard or young song-thrush preparing to fly
   Ere the pinions of flight had been reared.

The sun threw a flush o'er a burning rose-bush,
   And all idly the chrysalis hung,
For the gallant New Born, breathing love for the blush
   Of the rose, into giddy flight sprung ;
And so fondly he flew on the soft breeze that blew,
   That he reached with delight the loved flower :
As the soul of a bard a rich poem would view,
   And by flight should grow conscious of power.

And upon the sweet flower he enchanted the hour,
   And basked in her smile and the sun,   [dower,
And his bright wings displayed, with their rare coloured
   And the soft feathered down they had on.
The panting wings rich with red velvet were drest,
   And dark bars and white rings and light plumes ;
And enraptured he lay in his black, glossy vest,
   Like a genius whom glory illumes.

But a cloud hid the sun, and a storm shower came on,
  And the raindrops destroyed its bright dyes;
And its velvet was crape, and its scarlet was dun,
  And the tears dimmed its emerald eyes;
And its young breath was faint, and unheard was its
    plaint,
  And it died on the breast of the rose,
Like a genius too fair, at once martyr and saint,
  And whose glories have death for their close.

THE DAY OF WOMAN.

IT was the dewy morning of the world,—
It was the spring-tide of the human race,—
A gold and green-ringed spotted snake was curled
Around an infant's neck, in fond embrace ;
The full-maned lion lay beside the lamb ;
A fire-eyed, tawny panther in green bowers
Was to a milk-white fawn the foster dam ;
And Woman gathered Eden's odorous flowers.

It was the scorching noonday of our star,
Hot tropic summer suns oppressed the earth,
The beams of chivalry, like lances, far
Gleamed o'er a battle-field of blood and dearth :
The knight lay gasping through his steel-barred helm,
The squire lay white in death and stern in pride,
The king had fled his saddle and his realm ;—
But Woman watched her true-love knight beside !

It was the purple evening of the world,—
    At evening time there shall be blessed light !—
War's blood-red banner by fair Peace was furled,
    And brotherhood's clasped hands with rings were
        bright ;
Men's homes were beautiful and rich and high,
    And earth was bloomy through her grassy leas ;
And over all there was a solemn sky,
    And Woman sat, with children on her knees.

PRIMROSE TIME.

Birds begin their sweet spring lays,
  Hedges grow in young bright green,
Suns light showers up with their rays,
  Rainbows span the heavenly scene :
Everything is sweet and young,
  Everything is in its prime ;
Music chimes from every tongue,
  In primrose time—in primrose time !

Gauzy wings flit in the beam,
  Daisies bud amid the grass,
Butterflies of summer dream,
  And of May-day dreams the lass :
Everything is sweet and young,
  Everything is in its prime ;
Music chimes from every tongue,
  In primrose time—in primrose time !

Redder, lips ; eyes, brighter far ;
   Pulses warmer, fonder beat ;
Fairer shines the evening star,
   Lighter trip the fairies' feet :
Everything is sweet and young,
   Everything is in its prime ;
Music chimes from every tongue,
   In primrose time—in primrose time !

BREAD FROM BRAIN.

WHERE the iron of our lives
  Is wrought out in fire and smoke,
There the mighty Vulcan strives ;—
  Hot the furnace—hard the stroke !
There the windy bellows blow,
There the sparks in millions glow,
There, on anvil of the world,
Is the clanging hammer hurled.
    Hard the labour—small the gain,
    Is in making bread from brain !

Where that nameless stone is raised,
  There the Patriot's bones were placed :
Lived he—little loved and praised ;
  Died he—little mourned and graced !
There he sleeps who knew no rest,
There, unblest by those he blest :

P

Here he starved, while sowing seed ;—
Where he starved the worms now feed !
      Hard the labour—small the gain,
      Is in making bread from brain !

In that chamber, lone and drear,
      Sits a Poet, writing flowers,—
Bringing heaven to earth more near,—
      Raining thoughts in dewy showers :
While he sings of nectar rare
Only is the inkbowl there ;
Feasts divine he chaunts in trust
As he eats the mouldy crust !
      Hard the labour—small the gain,
      Is in making bread from brain !

When the Prophet's mourning voice
      Shouts the burden of the world,
Sackcloth-robes must be his choice,
      Ashes on his head be hurled :
Where the tyrants sit at ease,
Where false priests do as they please,
He is scorned and pierced in side,
He is stoned and crucified !
      Hard the labour—small the gain,
      Is in making bread from brain !

Patriot, poet, prophet, feed
   Only on the mouldy crust !
Tyrant, fool, and false priest, need
   All the crumb, and scorn the just !
Lord ! how long ?   How long, O Lord ?
Bless, O God, mind's unsheathed sword !
Let the pen become a sabre ;
Let Thy children eat who labour !
    Bless the labour—bless the gain,
    In the making bread from brain !

THE GOLD DIGGER.

Over the land and over the sea
She beckoned him with her fingers thin ;
Forth from the peace of a grassy lea,
Sung by the chimes of a sparkling linn :
And O, that lady was fair to see,
With golden locks, like bloom of the whin ;
So very bright in the distance, she—
  That lady fair with the golden hair—
The fairest dame he had ever seen !

Away from a quiet home, where love
Was training its honeysuckles fair,
With hands as pure as the white foxglove
Which grew with the heath and bracken there.
She had beckoned him from the clouds above,—
That lady fair with the golden hair,—
She had looked and smiled, and called him love,
And she shook at him her golden hair.

He followed her to a country strange,
Where the pathless track was salt and bare ;
Where the painted Indians far could range,
And the howling wolf-dogs had their lair :
And where clouds and waterfalls exchange,
Up high on the mountain's rugged stair,
He marked his tread with dark stains of red,
And followed her with the golden hair.

On by the torrent, and through the bush,
Thorny and matted, and parched for air,
Where the snake, hid by the crimson blush
Of trumpet flower, coiled its emerald snare ;—
Onward did he to the prairie push,
Where the Escholtzia's sunny glare,
And the orange light of blossoms bright
Glowed like that lady's golden hair.

Onward he went to a river bar,
Where there were working strange figures, bare,
Muddy, and marked with many a scar,
Delving in plashy holes, pair by pair :
" And O, have you seen," he cried, " my Star ;—
My golden-tressed love, and fairest fair ?
O tell," he cried, " where my love may hide,—
That lady with the golden hair !"

And at first they stared, and then they spoke,—
" Alas ! the lady is buried there !
Come and dig with us and you shall look
Upon her rich golden locks so rare !
Come, take a spade, and, true as a book,
Thou shalt raise her lovely body fair ;
For 'tis Wealth alone, all souls must own,
Is lady of the golden hair !"

He hearkened their voice,—those sordid men,—
And richer and richer grew his share ;
But he never saw his own again,
Nor met with the bracing mountain air,
Nor trod through his native Scottish glen :
For now he had naught of love to spare,
For the richer he, the more shone she,—
That lady with the golden hair.

Known at the mart, and known at the docks,—
He worked for her, and she did not care ;
Yet the more he piled his barley-shocks,
Gleamed brighter his syren's tresses fair ;
And the more he sheared his Spanish flocks,
Did those golden locks wave in the air,
And from her rock, with a merry mock,
She shook at him her golden hair.

But when, old and cold, he made his moan,
And skies were dull and the earth was bare,
Then this was the burden of his tone :—
" O, why did I leave my young love fair,
To follow far her who hears no groan,—
That dame whom I thought beyond compare,
Who beckoned me o'er the desert lone ;
That lady fair with the golden hair,
Who leaves me alone to turn to stone,—
That lady with false golden hair !"

A WINTER AFTERNOON.

THE sheeted snow-drifts by the hedges lie,
A yellow streak edges the western sky,
The chimneys send their azure wreaths on high.

Deep blue the church, the castle, and the town ;
Most deeply blue, as though imperial gown,
In purple state, flowed to the valley down.

All purple-blue, the castle stately lowers ;
Purple its walls, its battlements, its towers,
Serene in state as ancient princely hours.

And purple-blue—no more a line of fire,
But a wan finger—points the church's spire,
From its blent base to where white skies hang higher.

And purple-blue the house-roofs of the town,
Which cluster round the spired and castled crown
Of its old hill, and look thus mighty down.

And thro' such symbol-colouring, Bard may see
Religion, Rule, and Civic Liberty,
Each in its state robed right imperially.

Each having rightful empire ; each a part
Of sovereign sway over the human heart ;
In purple hue—that tower and spire and mart.

THE DANCE OF THE STARS.

THE bright moon dances round the earth,
  And fills our bards with songful measures ;
While round the sun, in whirling mirth,
  Three planets shake their locks' bright treasures.
Now advancing—now retiring,—
  In apogeè—in perigeè ;
Now their motions swiftly firing,—
  Now slow and stately dance the three :
Then to the east—then to the west—
  Round they turn, and round, and round,
Forming figures, without rest,
  O'er the blue celestial ground.
While amid the starry mazes
  Other fair sets form their dances,
Circling all with Beauty's blazes
  As the Ball of Night advances :

Thirty-three, all hand in hand,
 Wreathed in one high heavenly pleasure,
Joined in one bright beaming band,
 Step in time and move in measure.
Round the amorous star of Jove
 Four most fair ones dance with passion,
Trembling round him as they move,
 Circling sweet his jealous station :
While round dark old Saturn's orb,
 Seven sisters—each one vying
In the love that doth absorb—
 Are the dance of joy supplying.
And around how rich the singing !
 How it swells on poet's ear !
As when Endymion heard the ringing
 Of the moon's voice, crystal clear.
As they dance, the stars are singing,
 Tone and semi-tone are blending ;
Shafts of sound around are winging,
 Which their bows of voice are sending.
Hark ! great Jupiter's deep bass,
 Mingled with old Saturn's tones,
Fill the vaulted roofs of space, .
 Hush with solemn sounds our groans !
While brave Mars his tenor raises,
 And our Earth and Venus chime

Counter-tenor, in the praises
  Of each other, true in time ;
And the thrill of Mercury's treble
  Ravishingly ripples on
In the skyey streams, a pebble
  Liquid-sounding in its tone :
And all stars take up the chorus,
  Some with voice and some with string,
Till the spheral sounds come o'er us,
  And souls dance and spirits sing !

THE TIME OF DAY.

When morning red is raying,
      Then 'tis the time of day !
When children blithe are playing,
      Then 'tis the time of day !
When gentle lambs are feeding,
And lovely flowers are seeding,
And birds their songs are leading,
      Then 'tis the time of day !

When noontide suns are beaming,
      Then 'tis the time of day !
When schoolboys' eyes are gleaming,
      Then 'tis the time of day !
When kine rest in the meadows,
And earth has lost its shadows,
And sunbeams are God's ladders,
      Then 'tis the time of day !

When purple evening gloameth,
    Then 'tis the time of day !
When lad with lassie roameth,
    Then 'tis the time of day !
When sheep are folded meetly,
And flower-cups closed up neatly,
And nightingales sing sweetly,
    Then 'tis the time of day !

When starry night is shining,
    Then 'tis the time of day !
When moonbeams clouds are lining,
    Then 'tis the time of day !
When fireside jokes are springing,
And crickets blithe are singing,
And merry songs are ringing,
    Then 'tis the time of day !

Wherever loved is Nature,
    Then 'tis the time of day !
Wherever blest a creature,
    Then 'tis the time of day !
Whenever sin is shriven,
Whenever love is given,
Then earth's clock strikes from heaven,
    And 'tis the time of day !

AN AUTUMN AFTERNOON.

THE sun shines out upon the hills around,
And shedding radiance o'er the rising ground,
Each shade retreats to its own proper bound.

And there its note, in harmony of hue,
It meetly plays, to graver measure true,
Than livelier green or more transparent blue.

Which now the earth and now the sky adorn,
The dim mists, driven to the distance, lorn,—
The autumn afternoon a spring-like morn!

How sweet the green beneath the brightening track
Of the sun's radiance, and how fair the rack
Of those white clouds, amid their shower-friends black.

How pure the blue between those cloudlets there,
And their dark·brethren, whose wild raven hair,
By contrast show their curling locks more fair.

Ruddy the heather on the rising down,—
The withered ferns display a brighter brown,—
In the sun's smile the furze has lost its frown !

There, high the ridgy scar, in stern array,
By one clear line of light defends the way,
All fortified with walls of silver gray.

Slant from the sun deepen the shades, and oft
The bloom of blackness, darkness fair and soft,
Glows, clustering up the mountain sides, aloft.

While on each hill top glancing lustre glows,
Like burning tongues upon apostles' brows,
In council met to bless a world of woes.

And these, like them, in autumn or in spring,
Have but one teaching,—" Priests but shadows bring ;
Receive God's sunshine,—'tis a blessed thing !"

FAREWELL TO THE NORTH.

FAREWELL to the North!—to its cold healthy breezes,
Its moors and its hollows, its tarns and its fells;
To many a scene which fond Memory seizes,
And sun-painting keeps in its deepest of cells!
Its winds blow full cold, but they appetite strengthen;
Its hills they are steep, but the gorse blows thereon;
And the higher we climb shall the fair landscape
    lengthen,—
The longer remain in the mind when we're gone!

Farewell to the North! where the beck, brightly
    flowing,
Casts its white foamy flood o'er the wheel of the mill;
While the young flitting rainbows amid it are glowing,
And the showers of bright drops fall in musical trill!
Farewell to its streamlets, farewell to its rivers;
To the fair bed of Aire,—to the Crook of the Lune,—
To streams where the rush like a young bather shivers,
To the water-force working, yet gurgling its tune!

Q

Farewell to the North! where the moors in the even
Wear deepest of purple or richest of brown,
With gold of the sunset amid their robes weaven,
Under clouds taking shape from each mountainous
    crown;
Where the skirts of the fells are all red with the
    heather,
Or bright with the wild broom or gold with the whin,
And the flocks of the sky, in the changes of weather,
Drop down fleecy mists o'er their grass-browsing kin!

Farewell to the North!—to the land of the mountains,
To their deep quiet tarns, to their steep blackened sides,
Whence, like light amid darkness, the seams of bright
    fountains
Pour down with wild music their swift silver tides!
Though mountain to mountain shouts forth as to
    brother,
There are soft ferny clefts where true love may repose;
The heather bells ring marriage chimes to each other,
And cheeks blooming still tell of "Wars of the Rose."

Farewell to the North!   A fair farewell be given
To the pride of our England,—the Land of our
    Lakes,—

Where Windermere wanders,—the mirror of heaven!—
And many a harp to the poet awakes !
From the bright leaves of spring, from the autumn's
    rich-tinted,
The streams of faint melody flow on his ear ;
O'er the waters of Keswick they rise still unstinted,
And skim o'er the lake to the graves of Grasmere.

Farewell to the North ! When the Lord of Creation
Gave green linnet plumes and gave grey linnet song,
He said : " Let the South be a warm pleasant station :
Be the North bare above, but beneath, rich and
    strong !"
So the South, on its surface, has wheat waving golden,
To deck the tanned brow and the garner to fill :
Yet the brave gallant North has its arms never folden,
But, mining or weaving, to Labour adds Skill !

Farewell to the North! Though its children of Labour
Be rough and uncouth, or may seem so at first ;
Though cold to the stranger, they're warm to the
    neighbour,—
There are draughts at the beck that shall quench the
    heart's thirst !

There are Lancashire Witches no bogart can trouble ;
There's fern in the lane, but wild flowers ere it end ;
There's bright-bearded barley amid the dry stubble ;
There's a fist for a foe, but a hand for a friend !

Farewell to the North, then !—its lakes and its moun-
  tains,
Its moors and its hollows,—its best and its worst,—
Its tarns and its fells, and its streams and their foun-
  tains ;
There are draughts from its becks that can quench the
  soul's thirst !
Then here's to each friend ! and come, fill me a can full,
To hearts with deep founts whence the mountains
  stand forth ;
The rough, but the real, the warm and the manful ;
Here's health and farewell to all friends in the North !

THE OLD WALL.

Upon the shaded grey of that old wall,
Which long has marked the parklands of yon hall,
What painted glories where the broad lights fall !

The mosses, richly golden and dark green,
With deep red patches here and there between,
Lit up, glow forth, and blaze the stony screen.

And as when virtuous age erectly stands,
Blazoned by all its deeds, and rich in lands,
The painter's wealth of colour it commands :

So, that grey wall is rich with colours bright ;
So, with grouped mosses, gold and red, 'tis dight ;
So, o'er it spreads a glowing breadth of light.

The good old cause of right,—the ancient spirit
That calmly stood in confidence of merit,—
The blazons of that rich old wall inherit.

The bygone ages—pages in the story
That history tells in graven words of glory—
Are thus kept verdant, like that old wall hoary.

And may the Bard no sadder fate befall
Than in old age forth coloured life to call,
Like the rich mosses o'er that grey old wall !

THE LAST GREEK BARD'S SONG
OF HOMER.

BRING me, boy, the Samian flask,
  Sound thy flute beneath those trees,
While at ease my limbs I bask
  Where the myrtles woo the breeze :
Bring the tablets, ink, and reed,
  Homer sang here ages past ;
Echo's sacred grots may lead
  To his fount of song at last.

Bright the blue Egean flows,
  Tempe's vale is rich with bloom ;
Scented Hybla sweeter grows,
  And Ilissus hallows gloom ;
But though blue the skies above,
  And though green the earth below,
Have they brought us, in their love,
  Father Homer's tuneful flow ?

Fair the Academic groves,
   Life-like statues there we see,
Marbled virtues, graces, loves,—
   All but moving symmetry :
Yet not statues, but true men
   Still we want, and, singing, pray—
Bring us Homer back again,
   Such may live to swell his lay.

Proud the dames of Athens move,
   Lone in wealth and slaves of state ;
Listless in the terraced grove,
   Poor in love and weak in hate :
Stately formed, and decked with art,
   Jewelled though their armlets be,
Are they worthy Homer's heart ?
   He who sung Penelope !

Have we women ?   Have we men ?
   Men we have, and women, too ;—
Look upon them once again,
   Scarce the different sex you know !
Men we have for whom the helm
   Weighs too heavy on the brow ;—
Did such aid, in Homer's realm,
   Achilles' wrath, or Hector's woe ?

Barbaric hordes press on our soil,
    And swords are pointed, not to save ;
In ease inglorious is our toil,
    We have no strength to earn a grave.
The bard has fallen on evil days,
    And Homer will not leave the tomb,
When life has lost its crown of bays,
    And death's urns tell no noble doom.

Then break the tablets, break the reed,
    Though Greece is fair in earth and sky,
Though rich the Marathonian mead
    With blood whose fame can never die !
In vain we strive as bards to sing ;—
    Unless we first can show us men
The Gods no inspiration bring,
    Nor send us Homer back again.

But though we to barbarians fall,
    Like temple to the bats, a prey,
I have one hope,—the last of all,—
    It is in our old Homer's lay ;
While it survives our Greece will live,
    The land of a most glorious lyre,
And unborn laureled poets give
    Our prince of bards a crown of fire !

THE YOUTH AND FAME.

WITHIN a study, small and dimly lighted,
Like a faint tapering torch burnt low and blighted,
Sat a fair youth, in ancient lore benighted.

To him a vision, radiant as fresh flame,
In a new-kindled burning roseblush came;
She named herself not, but a voice cried Fame!

" Why art thou here, poor sleeping one ?" she said ;
" Why use the pillow of another's head ?
Awake, poor sleeper, slumbering on the dead !"

" I am awake," to her the youth replied ;
" I slumber not,—my soul is open-eyed,—
Morning is ever, and night's sleep denied !"

"If so," said she, "why borrow from another?
The light is given to thee as to thy brother;
Thou sleep'st in day and dost thy daydreams smother."

"Behold my answer!" said the youth; "behold
Those radiant reams which unto me are gold,
To others dross! Canst thou their leaves unfold?"

"I can," said Fame, "for unto me are given
St. Peter's keys, when genius seeks for heaven!
But thee I know but with the Sleepers Seven!"

"But yet my dream," said he, "hath wings, and flies
Over the heads of thousands, to whose eyes
The eagle flight hath often auguries."

"How know I that?" said she; "a yellow bill
May be that bird's who yields thee not a quill;—
Thou soarest not, but peckest the blind worm still!

"The eagle, launching from its mountain dun,
Spreads its own wings, like sails, the air upon,
Breasts cloud and storm, and looks in the face the sun.

"Its eyes are dazed not by its fiery beam ;
It sees the earth a speck on which men dream ;
It flaps its wings, and shrieks a long shrill scream.

"Then thro' a flight of clouds it sees in the breeze
A hillock white,—the Alps and Pyrenees,—
And a blue lake,—the breathless, waveless seas.

"Then swooping downward, like a blast of wind,
Or seer from heaven sent unto mankind,
Men stare all-eye, and God restores the blind.

"But thou, poor sleeper, hast no eagle flight ;
Thy pinions are the webs of dreams by night,
Than rainbow woof of gossamer more light."

"Saidst thou, 'Awake'?" the dreaming poet said ;
" I will arise, nor slumber with the dead,   `
The sun is blushing and the east is red."

" Up, then !" said she, " **the** will can ever claim
The birth of deed.   Rise heavenward, like flame,"
She said, and all the air resounded " Fame !"

"O mighty One!" exclaimed the youth, "I think,
I soar above the world's tenebrious brink,
And of the eternal ocean's waters drink!

"I feel wings grow! I feel the powers of flight!
I rise! I float! and, with a glorious might,
Sail over clouds to where there is no night!

"Thy words have blown me breezes swift and strong;
I mount the spheres, and, breathing free and long,
I soar thus to the sunny realms of song!"

THE HAND OF FRIENDSHIP.

———◆———

GIVE me the hand that is warm, kind, and ready,
Give me the clasp that is calm, true, and steady;
Give me the hand that will never deceive me,
Give me its grasp that my soul may believe thee!
  Soft is the palm of the delicate woman,
  Hard is the hand of the rough sturdy yeoman:
  Soft palm or hard hand it mattereth never,
  Give me the grasp that is friendly for ever!

Give me the hand with the grasp of a brother;
Give me the hand that has harmed not another;
Give me the hand that has never forsworn it,—
Give me its grasp that my love may adorn it!
  Lovely the palm of the fair blue-veined maiden,
  Horny the hand of the workman o'erladen:
  Soft palm or hard hand it mattereth never,
  Give me the grasp that is friendly for ever!

U N I T Y.

Existence is composed of circles, all
In one great circle, and the centre—God.
There is one common life for star and clod,—
The clouds which rise, again in rain must fall.
All things are one, in progress and in end ;
And as the individual man must be
Free to form part of free society,
Before in truth he calls the king his friend,
So must each nation, crowned with liberty
As with a glory, dwell in its own light,
By others hindered not ; until, God-led,
Of its own free will it longeth to be wed,
And joineth hands with others.   Glorious sight !
One world, one people, and one common Head !

JOHN HAMER, PRINTER, LEEDS.

www.ingramcontent.com/pod-product-compliance
Lightning Source LLC
Chambersburg PA
CBHW020055030726
47498CB00006B/1800